MURDER AND HIGH ROLLERS

A High Desert Cozy Mystery - Book 10

BY

DIANNE HARMAN

Published by: Dianne Harman
www.dianneharman.com

Interior, cover design and website by
Vivek Rajan

ISBN: 9781712507926

CONTENTS

ACKNOWLEDGMENTS

My husband and I recently spent a few days at Pechanga Resort, a Native American casino in Temecula, California. In addition to having a superb golf course, so my husband says, it has one of the largest gaming casinos I've ever seen. When we were walking around in it, I noticed a poker room for "high rollers," but almost no one was in it.

I couldn't stop thinking about the high rollers room. Who plays there? Where are they from? Do they win or lose? The Muse, as I call the creative spirit, had taken over, and I had to write the book.

Thank you, Pechanga, and thanks to the people who shared their gambling stories with me. I hope you enjoy the read as much as I enjoyed the write!

And to all the people responsible for making sure my books get to market – from the technical computer processes to making sure the books are error free – I hope you know how very much I appreciate each and every one of you!

And to Tom, as always, thanks for being my support.

PROLOGUE

Lance Kendrick was on cloud nine. There was nothing, absolutely nothing, like walking out of a casino card room $600,000 richer. Usually he let his winnings stay with the casino, but this time was different. He'd seen the perfect diamond engagement ring for Shania, and although he wasn't going to use anywhere near all of his winnings on it, he was definitely going to use a substantial portion of them to buy it for her.

He thought about calling her, but it was 4:15 a.m. in Las Vegas, and he knew she'd be sound asleep and not too thrilled to be awakened, although if he told her about his winnings, that would probably take a lot of the sting out of it. He decided he'd wait until he knew she'd be up, getting ready for her last week as a cocktail waitress at the Las Vegas casino where she worked. Then she'd be joining him in Palm Springs.

Lance was glad he'd decided to come to Palm Springs. Most of the casinos in Las Vegas and a few other places had expressed their feelings that he was no longer welcome in their casinos. Lance couldn't help it if he had an eidetic memory, which is a fancy medical term for someone like him who has a photographic memory.

And he couldn't help it that it was as if he had a computer in his brain, a computer that not only remembered every card that had been dealt, but a computer that instantly calculated the chances of what card would be dealt next.

Lance had first discovered his unusual brain condition and how it worked to his benefit in card games when he was in high school. He and some of his friends had played poker and Lance had cleaned them out. Of course, cleaning out teenage boys meant that he won a total of $100. But that was the last time Lance ever walked away from a card game with that little amount of money.

He'd begun to gamble seriously after high school since some states had set the minimum legal age for gambling at eighteen. His parents had desperately wanted him to go to college, but he knew he could make more in a few months than he'd ever make with a college degree, and so it had begun.

The next few years were spent going from one casino to another. He went down the East Coast as himself, but when the casinos began to ID him, he reversed and went up the east coast wearing various kinds of disguises. When he was no longer welcome, in disguise or not, at the East Coast casinos, he started to frequent the Midwest casinos. And so it went, casino to casino. He kept traveling west, having worn out his welcome in Las Vegas, Reno, and other well-known gambling venues.

It had been several years now, and Lance was gambling on the West Coast, mainly at the California Indian casinos, of which there were many. Being a pragmatic man, and knowing that his welcome would be up at some point at those casinos as well, he'd begun to research the casinos in Hong Kong and Macao. He'd decided that's where he and Shania should be married. That way, none of his family would be able to attend the wedding, and given their thoughts on his choice of an occupation, it was probably just as well.

When he was playing cards, he had no appetite, but now he was starving. People who saw him win big, probably thought he celebrated with a huge filet mignon and all the trimmings, but the truth was, at heart he was still just a little boy from a small town in West Virginia. A peanut butter and jelly sandwich with chips and a big glass of milk was all he wanted.

Lance was in his hotel room and had just taken his first bite when he heard a knock on the door. He looked through the security peephole in the door and recognized someone from the card game at the casino. He opened the door and said "Hello."

The person standing on the other side of the door was holding a bottle of champagne and said "Just wanted to congratulate you on tonight's winnings." He extended his hand to shake Lance's hand and Lance automatically gripped the person's handshake. The person turned around and hurried away, closing the door on Lance, who had slumped to the floor.

Unfortunately, the hand that shook Lance's had a fentanyl patch in it and the powerful drug immediately went into Lance's nervous system. His breathing slowed and he struggled to stand up, as the fentanyl exacerbated his asthma, causing him to have extreme difficulty in breathing.

It would have been wise of Lance to call 9-1-1, but instead his first thought was of Shania. He called her and in a raspy, catching voice said, "I…need…help. Someone…from…the…card…game…

"Lance, what's wrong? Lance? Lance, talk to me."

When there was no response, she ended the call and placed a call to the Palm Springs Police Department. She hysterically told them what had happened and asked that someone go to the room where Lance was staying at the hotel casino. The dispatcher immediately sent the police and an ambulance to the hotel casino.

Minutes later the EMT's had Lance in an ambulance, but it was too late. Even with an infusion of oxygen, he died on the way to the hospital. The police, suspecting foul play, began a systematic search of his hotel room and discovered his wallet with a check in it payable to Lance Kendrick in the amount of $600,000.

When they completed their search, they sealed off the room with crime scene yellow tape. They impounded Lance's clothing and personal effects, including his cell phone.

At 5:00 a.m. Detective Jeff Combs, the head of the homicide division of the Palm Springs Police Department, was awakened with the news that Lance had died and his death, according to the police on the scene, appeared to be a homicide. Jeff carefully got out of bed so he wouldn't wake his wife, Marty, and left for the Palm Springs police station.

As the head of the homicide division, it was Jeff's sad responsibility to call the woman named Shania and give her the bad news. Informing loved ones that someone was deceased was definitely at the bottom of his enjoyment list.

CHAPTER ONE

For many years, Joannie Lambert had been a household name. During the last thirty years, her face was always on one or more of the tabloids next to the grocery store checkout stand. She'd done it all, and it was all very well documented. Of course, when you have a good public relations team, that's not too hard to do.

Affairs, marriages, rehabs, plastic surgeries, public spats, and vacations on yachts owned by Mid-East sheikhs were just a few of the things for which she was well known. Unfortunately, at some point in time, nature will have its way, and nature had come calling on Joannie at the ripe old age of fifty-eight. Although she'd had a lot of work done over the years trying to keep nature at bay, this time she made a deal with the devil in the form of a facelift that the doctor said would take thirty years off of her face.

He lied. In his nervousness to make a name for himself by doing Joannie Lambert's face, he'd botched the job and botched it badly. Joannie didn't look thirty years younger, if anything, she looked thirty years older. And there was a very limited market for women who looked eighty-eight, be it as marriage material, movie material, or television material. The only other market available was doing ads for adult diapers, and that was something she refused to do no matter how lucrative her agent said it would be.

The other thing the facelift was good for was being a poster child for why one shouldn't get a facelift from doctors who promise you'll look thirty years younger, and Joannie had no desire to see herself in the tabloids looking as she did now.

Even with all her fame and fortune, most of which had been spent, Joannie was still a very practical woman. Practical enough to leave Hollywood and buy a condominium in a Palm Springs development which had a casino attached to it. She'd always been good at playing poker and other card games and decided this was a way she could make some money, and at the same time, have some fun now that she was retired.

She didn't want to play with the people who came to Palm Springs to attend a convention or were tourists on a family vacation. After all, she was Joannie Lambert, and Joannie Lambert wouldn't stoop to play cards with the common people.

One of her reasons for buying a condo in this particular development, which was attached to a well-known Native American casino, was the high stakes poker game the casino had. It cost $25,000 just to buy in. She figured if she won as much as she lost, she could play for a long time. What she hadn't planned on was losing several nights in a row to a man from China and then the last two nights to some guy who said he was from West Virginia.

This was not working out at all as Joannie had planned. She'd only been playing two weeks, and she was already down several hundred thousand dollars, far more money than she could afford to lose. Then one day, while she was having a late lunch, she was reading the paper and happened to see her horoscope.

She read it and reread it. "Tonight, all you wish shall be yours. Be not hesitant." She took a sip of her coffee and thought about what it could mean. After several moments of consideration, Joannie was sure this was a sign that tonight she should go for broke. If that West Virginia guy was in the game, after what he'd won last night, it really was time for his luck to change.

The more she thought about it, the more convinced she was that her time had come. She spent the afternoon and evening getting ready for her big win. She went to the bank and withdrew $200,000, sure that tomorrow she'd be making a deposit of at least $400,000.

Promptly at midnight, when the private card room reserved for high stakes poker players opened, she was ushered in and seated. She looked around and saw that she was the only woman there. She recognized the Chinese man who had been on a lucky streak until the West Virginia man, who was also there, had begun playing. Other than that, she didn't recognize the other players.

She smiled at everyone. She could afford to be magnanimous, because she knew how the game was going to go. She'd win big.

Poor Joannie. It was a nice pipe dream, but several hours later she found it wasn't reality. When the game ended, she'd lost $200,000, money she could ill afford to lose. A trouper to the end, she smiled at the men at her table, picked up her purse and walked to where the red rope closed off the room to members of the general public.

"Good night, Richard," she said with a smile to the guard as he unlooped the rope and let her through. She walked through the casino and down the hall to the elevators, not believing what had just happened.

As soon as she'd let herself into her condominium, she walked over to the bar and poured herself a stiff vodka on the rocks. An occasional glass of vodka was a habit she'd gotten into in her early years in Hollywood. She'd overheard two actors talking about vodka and how, unlike some other spirits, it was impossible to smell it on someone's breath and it didn't show up in the form of wrinkles on the face. From then on, she'd been a fan.

Joannie knew she was in shock. She may have lost intermittently to the Chinese man over the last few weeks when he was playing in the room, but this was the second night in a row she'd lost to the man from West Virginia. The more she thought about it, the madder she got and the more certain she was that somehow, he was cheating. No one could win that consistently.

She never drank alcohol when she was playing cards, but she wasn't playing cards right now, and the vodka had become her friend. After the third drink, it assured her she was right, the man had to be cheating, and something should be done about it.

The alcohol even had the audacity to remind Joannie that she had some fentanyl patches in her bathroom cabinet that had been given to her after her facelift by her doctor for pain. A couple of patches would be enough to make sure the West Virginia man never sat at another gaming table.

And the vodka went on to remind her that she knew his room number because she'd seen him charge his drink to his room, room number 475, just a short distance from her condo's location. She heard it urging her to hurry, before she lost her nerve, and tomorrow night would be different. Tomorrow night she would be the big winner.

CHAPTER TWO

"Seriously? The tribe asked you to appraise some of their things?" Marty's sister, Laura asked.

"Not exactly. It was your boss, Dick. He said the most important artifacts the tribe has are displayed in a high stakes card room at the casino. He's afraid they're really undervalued and wants me to take a look at them. From what he said, the room is off limits to the general public and only the really, really wealthy high rollers have access to it. It has a guard standing by a red velvet rope that bars entry, and it's guarded 24/7."

"Well, since I'm not a really, really wealthy high roller, that certainly lets me out. I'll just have to take your word about how fabulous the pieces are." Laura reached down to pet Marty's two dogs who were fast asleep at her feet.

Patron, the white boxer, who seemed to share Laura's psychic abilities and Duke, the aging black Lab, loved to spend time during the day in the courtyard when any of the members of the loosely called "commune" were at home.

"Marty," Laura said in an ominous tone, "I feel the need to tell you something."

"Just once, Laura, could you please not say anything about an appraisal that I'm excited about, but one that you're getting vibes about. I don't think that's asking too much."

"It's probably not, but the good news is that you're not in danger, at least not now."

"Gee, Laura, you don't know how good that makes me feel," Marty said sarcastically. "And what else is my sister the psychic getting? Oh, and is Patron on the same wavelength you are? What's he getting?"

"Please lose the attitude, Marty. This has nothing to do with me. I'm simply a vessel that things flow through. You know I can't help any of it. I don't like the fact that they want you to do this appraisal from midnight to 4:00 a.m. It doesn't make me feel good."

"To be honest, I'm not real nuts about that part, but I didn't have a choice."

"Why not?" Laura asked.

"Dick told me that this is a very exclusive private card room reserved for the highest rollers who play high stakes poker. It's only open from midnight to 4:00 a.m. There are three guards in the room at that time, and since the artifacts I'll be appraising are worth a great deal of money, they wanted me there when the guards are there.

"He also said that one of the guards would be assigned to me exclusively. He'd meet me at my car when I got there and escort me back to it when I'm finished for the night."

"I'd think having you there would detract from the players' concentration," Laura said.

"From what I was told, gamblers at this level are so focused on what they're doing, because the stakes are so high, they won't even know I'm in the room. Plus, like I said, the rest of the time the glass display doors are locked and there's a guard posted outside of the room, around the clock. No one is allowed in there other than between the hours of midnight and 4:00 a.m."

"I'd think there's also a strong message that they're too cheap to have a guard or two there during the day so you could do your appraisal at a normal time."

Marty was quiet for a few moments and then said, "That wasn't specifically said, but I suppose one could infer it."

"And what does Jeff think about you doing an appraisal at that time of night?"

Marty looked away from her and said, "Well, he doesn't know about it. There was a homicide and he had to leave really early this morning. I haven't had a chance to tell him."

"I'm sure he'll just be thrilled about it," Laura said sarcastically.

"Now who has the attitude? Anyway, remember I'll have a guard with me from the time I get there until the time I leave," Marty said.

"Okay, sorry. Here's the thing. I'm getting some bad vibes about all of this. The murder he's working on now has something to do with your appraisal. That's all I'm getting at the moment."

"Thanks. I'll keep it in mind. I start tonight, so I'm going to drive down to the casino and take a look at the room. Once I get an idea of what they have, I can do some auction research on similar items. See you at dinner."

She stood up and walked towards her house, flanked on either side by Patron and Duke.

Well, at least Patron didn't flip out, like he usually does if Laura senses something. That's encouraging. Maybe this will go better than Laura thinks it will.

CHAPTER THREE

Diego Ramirez looked at the name on his cell phone screen and winced. "Lupe, I'll be back in a minute. I need to take this call in private," he said to the beautiful blond woman who was stretched out on a lounge next to the swimming pool.

"No problem, Diego. I'm not moving. This is the best. As a matter of fact, I may stay here the rest of my life. I'm so glad you asked me to move in with you."

He hurried into the house and walked back to his office. "This is Diego," he said as he closed the door behind him.

"My friend, this is John Chen. I think we need to talk."

"Yes, John, but this really isn't a good time for me. Let's do it later today."

"No. The $100,000 I paid you tells me it's a very good time for both of us. Diego, what is going on? I paid you a king's ransom to false shuffle and look what's happened. Some yahoo from West Virginia's been cleaning up."

"John, you did very well for several days. In fact, you got your $100,000 back many, many times over. As far as the guy from West Virginia? I don't know what's up with him."

"Well, let's put it this way. You better find out what's going on with him. You have two days, or I'll expect my $100,000 to be repaid with interest and our deal of $50,00 being paid to you every two weeks is off. If it's not repaid, I have friends who will make sure that it is.

"Oh, by the way, how does Lupe like that diamond ring you gave her? The one I paid for and the one that I'll take from her along with her ring finger if you don't make the problem go away. Don't think Lupe would look too good missing a finger. Oh well, you know how it goes. Accidents happen, right? I'll be in touch," John said as he ended the call.

Diego put the phone down and put his head in his hands. How had he ever gotten into this mess? At first everything was wonderful. He had Lupe, he could afford to buy her any piece of jewelry she wanted, he was making very good money at the casino. Yeah, everything was great. And now…

John had been very clear when he'd first approached Diego about exactly what he wanted from him and what he was willing to pay. The agreement had been $50,000 every two weeks for Diego to false shuffle when John or any of his associates were at his table when he was dealing. That was it. Very simple and straightforward.

Diego had felt like he'd grabbed the golden ring, because that was a piece of cake for him. Before Diego had become a dealer and he was learning the game of poker, the man who had taught him how to play had also taught him how to spot a dealer who was doing a false shuffle and how to do a false shuffle.

He'd become very, very good at it, even if he'd never used it at his table until his deal with John. The person who'd taught him said that it normally was used in baccarat, but could be used in poker as well. It involved the dealer shuffling cards so that they maintained a pre-arranged order.

The goal was to create a group of cards that appeared in the exact same order as when they were put in the discard tray. The players who knew what the dealer was doing could track the cards and increase or lower their bets depending on what cards were coming up next.

It required the dealer to look like he was actually shuffling the deck, but in reality, he was using a series of false shuffles to keep cards in their discard tray order. The player who is aware of the false shuffle is able to track card values since they're dealt to him under the guise of his being a "trend bettor," a player who adjust his bets based on previous outcomes.

Diego knew it was very difficult to detect a false shuffle when a really good dealer was doing it, and he only used it when John or one of his associates was playing. So far it had worked out well. But that had been before the West Virginian.

He couldn't figure out how the West Virginian had won so big. He was sure the pit boss had brought it to the attention of management, but if Diego hadn't spotted anything, he was sure the pit boss hadn't either. And when the pit boss spent time at his table, he would secretly signal towards John or his associate to let them know he couldn't false shuffle. The pit boss might spot it.

John and his men were very aware if they only won at Diego's table, and only when he was dealing during his forty-minute shifts, not when his replacement was there, it would be too noticeable. They were careful to lose from time to time, but overall, they were winners, big winners.

Diego sat for a long time and considered his options, which were seemingly slim and none. If he was going to keep Lupe, he needed John's money, and he wasn't willing to give her up. That meant something had to be done to the man from West Virginia so that he never played poker at Diego's table again.

It had been a long time since Diego had left the streets of East Los Angeles and his gang ties. He had no desire to go back to that way of life, but if something threatened this new life that he'd so carefully made, he wasn't afraid to use what he'd learned all those years ago.

He knew West Virginia's room number because he'd seen him sign the bar bills with it, room 475. Diego didn't like what he was thinking, but he felt he had no choice. Something would have to happen to the man, and Diego just happened to have something that would work. And he knew West Virginia would open the door to his room for him. It should be easy and then his life would be back on track.

CHAPTER FOUR

Mark Cohen was a professional gambler, pure and simple. He'd known from the first time he'd bet a kid in nursery school that it would rain the next day and he'd won the kid's snack, that his future was set.

To him, gambling was a miracle that brought him about anything he wanted. He was the first boy his age in high school to have a brand-new car. Mark knew he'd never forget the look on the salesman's face when at age sixteen he'd written a check for the full price of the car, $18,735.43. It was an amount he'd never forget.

Although he thought gambling was a miracle, his parents felt otherwise. His brother and sister had both gone to college and then on to graduate schools. Mark wanted none of it. He knew he could make more money in a couple of years than they'd make in ten years, plus his father had always used the fact that he'd paid for their education to make them very beholden to him.

When Mark turned twenty-one, he left home and had never looked back. His relationship with his family was tenuous at best and amounted to nothing more than a couple of phone calls a year from wherever he happened to be in the United States at that time. Even though he owned a 3,000 square foot condominium in Las Vegas, a Ferrari, a multi-million-dollar stock portfolio, and a part interest in a professional basketball team, in his family's eyes he was a failure.

Mark had finally accepted that unless he went to college and got a degree, he might as well write them off. Their existing relationship was as good as it was going to get.

Instead, he'd taken solace in the fact that he was one of the best gamblers around. Sure, there were others who would get on a hot streak and beat him from time to time, but overall, he was one of the absolute best in the United States.

At least he had been until he'd run across Lance at a casino a couple of years ago in Atlantic City, New Jersey. He'd cleaned Mark out. Unfortunately, like a bad penny, from time to time when Mark sat down at a table, there would be Lance, and he always, always won. Mark knew he could walk away from a table if Lance was playing, but his pride wouldn't let him. And every time he played with Lance, he lost.

It was beginning to get to him. Lance always acknowledged him with a nod of his head, ever the complete gentleman. Mark wondered what it would take to ruffle Lance. To get him so ruffled that he'd lose his concentration and start losing.

What if his family found out that some guy always beat Mark, no matter where they were playing? Mark wondered if Lance was trailing him, because lately he'd been showing up at the tables in whatever city Mark happened to be in, and Mark moved around a lot. Casinos got nervous when someone started winning too much. Some suggested that he find another casino. Some had sent scary looking men who looked like they'd be at home in the Mafia to his room with the same suggestion.

He wondered if they did the same to Lance? Maybe that's why he and Lance kept running into one another. He didn't know how Lance always won when they played, but he did. He never saw anything that led him to believe that Lance was cheating. Maybe he was just a better player than Mark.

Gambling was the only thing Mark had ever been successful at, not that he'd really tried to broaden his horizons. He loved what he did, and he loved what it had given him. He'd always been confident in his gambling abilities, and quite frankly, felt that was part of the reason he always won. The unshakeable certainty that he was better than anyone else drew the elements of success to him.

But for the first time in his career his confidence was really, really shaken when he'd seen Lance walk up to his table in the casino in Palm Springs. Mark knew Lance would win that night, and so he had. The one thing he'd always had going for him, and what Mark was certain was the key to his gambling success, his confidence, had been stolen by Lance.

As Mark thought about what was happening, he became angry, very, very angry. How dare this backwoods hillbilly from West Virginia show him up? Mark knew if Lance was gone, if he never had to see Lance again, his confidence would return and he'd be on top again – a winner.

As much as he didn't like what he was thinking, he finally admitted to himself that the only way to make certain Lance was permanently out of the picture was to do just that. Do away with Lance for good.

Mark shuddered at the thought of what he would have to do to make that a reality. He knew he was squeamish and the very thought of handling some type of a weapon just about made him throw up.

Then he remembered a television show he'd seen recently about an opioid called fentanyl. It was about how a man had murdered another man by giving him an overdose of it through a patch. A few months earlier Mark had been experiencing severe headaches and a doctor had given him numerous tests to try and determine the cause. The doctor suspected it might be a brain tumor. But all of the tests had come back negative, so the doctor had given him a prescription for fentanyl patches to deal with the pain.

Well, if I'm going to do this, I can get the prescription the doctor gave me and just increase the dosage of one of the patches by adding to it from the fentanyl in another patch, just like I saw on television. That would be pretty easy to do.

Heck, I could even have a bottle of champagne in my other hand and he'd think I was bringing him a peace offering. Yeah, this is definitely the way to go, Mark thought. *And then I'll be on top again.*

CHAPTER FIVE

Lily Chen whirled around when John ended his call and said, "Did you fix it?"

"Lily, I'm trying, believe me I'm trying. I called Diego and told him he better take care of that Lance guy, or not only would he not be getting any more money, he wouldn't be able to spend it even if he did."

"I've spent all morning arranging for our people to play at Diego's table for the next week, but the way Lance is winning, it's pointless. John, he's going to win every cent we've so carefully built up the last few months."

"I know, Lily, I know, and believe me, I'm just as worried about it as you are."

"John, the guy flits from casino to casino and town to town. We've got a lot of the dealers in our pocket because of what we've paid them to do the false shuffle, but if he goes to one of the casinos where our people are playing, it doesn't matter. Not only do we lose the money our person is gambling with, we also lose the money we paid to the dealer to make sure we'd win."

"What do you want me to do? That guy is like some human computer. Nobody who has played against him can find any tell or clue that he's cheating, but he has to be. No one can be that lucky or that robotic. I have no idea what's up with him."

"I'll tell you what I want you to do. I want you to get rid of him. He's threatening to ruin everything we've worked so hard to build up. I've recruited ten players, all loyal to us, and all fully on board with our plan. We use two of them each night at different casinos, and when Lance isn't around, it's all gravy."

"But the problem is, we never know where he's going to be," John said, finishing her sentence.

"Exactly. So what's the point in training these people if he's going to show up and ruin everything? Keep in mind that the ten people we now have doesn't include the three people we had to get rid of because they lost too much money to him, and they knew too much about us."

"I'm well aware of that, Lily. Believe me, this situation is not making me happy."

"John, we've been very lucky. No one knows about the three people. Fortunately, the cities where they were taken care of all had lakes. The authorities don't dredge lakes without a reason, and so far, there hasn't been a reason. Since their relatives all live in China, there were no missing person reports about them filed."

"Trust me, you're not telling me anything new. As a matter of fact, I've thought of little else besides how we can get rid of Lance. What concerns me is that the more people we get rid of, the more chances there are for mistakes to happen.

"Don't forget," John continued, "we used that man named Kang to take care of those three people, but even though we paid him well for taking care of them, someone could trace it to us because he was hired by us."

"Yes, John, but your uncle was the one who sent him here from China. I don't think he'll turn in his own nephew and you said your uncle had used him for years. Plus, he never saw us."

"I know, but how long do we just continue doing this, Lily? Sooner or later, we'll be caught. It's just a matter of time."

"John, you just answered your own question. Yes, if we continue doing away with people because they lose to this Lance person, there is a good chance we will get caught. And the more times we bring Kang here, the more times we run the risk of being caught. We need to take matters in our own hands. We didn't come this far only to have it taken from us."

"Well, since you seem to have thought this out, what do you propose we do?"

"Remember when I had breast cancer?"

"Of course, my love. How could I ever forget the darkest days of my life?"

"Well, one time when I was at the doctor's office and the pain was really bad, I asked him to give me something to deal with it. He gave me an opioid called fentanyl. It's really, really powerful. As a matter of fact, just a small amount too much can cause death. I never took it, but I still have it."

"Lily, what are you suggesting?"

"I'm not suggesting, I'm telling you that you need to pay the West Virginia hillbilly a call at his room, shake his hand with the fentanyl patch I'll make, and our troubles will be over. Fortunately, his death will be very, very fast."

"I don't think I can do that," John said. "We need to come up with something else."

"John, I'm not asking you to do this. I'm telling you to do this. And let's put it this way. If you haven't taken care of him within twenty-four hours, I will. I'll put a fentanyl patch that's double strength next to your sink in the bathroom."

"Lily, I can't do this. I really can't."

Lily looked at him and took a deep breath. "John, there's something I haven't told you. There's been a reoccurrence of my breast cancer. As a matter of fact, it's rather serious, as in life-threatening. I'm waiting for the results of some additional tests, and if they confirm what the doctor suspects, we may have to go back to China immediately."

"What do you mean?"

"I mean there's a good chance that I will have to have a mastectomy, possibly a double mastectomy. That would be in addition to chemotherapy or radiation, assuming the doctors think that would be effective. And they're worried it may have spread to other areas of my body.

"If that's so, I want to be treated in China, so I can have my family around me. I really didn't want to tell you, but that's the reason I've been working so hard to get our people ready. I knew there was a chance that I would have to spend my energy recuperating from surgery, rather than training people how to use the false shuffle."

"Lily, Lily, how can this be? You told me the doctor said you were in remission," John said, tears welling up in his eyes.

"For a long time, I was. You had so much on your mind I didn't want to burden you with anything else. But let's keep an optimistic outlook about my health. Maybe the tests and the x-rays were someone else's and he'll look at the new tests and tell me I'll be fine."

"When will you know the results?" he asked.

"Anytime. Actually, the doctor said it could be late tonight. He asked the lab to do the work on an emergency basis, but he called a while ago to tell me that I'd been bumped back a bit because the police had sent several tests to the lab that they wanted done immediately. The doctor told me that anything the police want done is a priority."

"Oh, Lily, I can't believe this. I thought all of this was behind us. Lily, I promise I'll take care of the problem we spoke of earlier. Don't even think about it. I want you to use every bit of energy you have available to heal yourself. I have several meetings and then the card game tonight, but I'll take care of that matter directly after the game."

"I know how busy you are John. Don't worry about me. Rather than try and interrupt your meetings, and I know they don't allow phones to be turned on in the card room, I'll text you when I hear something from the doctor. Check your phone when you have a chance and we'll decide what to do, if we need to do anything, tomorrow."

"Lily, if you want me to cancel the meetings and the card games, I will. I'd be happy to stay here with you and wait for the doctor's call."

"No, hopefully your luck will change tonight."

"My luck may not change tonight, but the man from West Virginia's luck is certainly going to change. Consider it one less thing you need to worry about, and Lily," he said as he walked over to her and took her face in her hands. "Just know how much I love you and that I'll be with you every minute during this. You won't have to do anything alone."

"I love you too, John. That's why I didn't want to tell you. I didn't want to worry you. And I'm glad you're getting rid of our other problem," she said as she gently kissed him.

CHAPTER SIX

Marty wanted to preview the location of the appraisal she was scheduled to conduct late that night, so she drove to the casino which was located in the downtown area of Palm Springs. The tribe who owned the casino also owned a majority of the land in Palm Springs. As the city became a winter time mecca for snowbirds from the northern states and Canada, the tribe had profited immensely. It was one of the wealthiest Native American tribes in the United States.

She parked her car in the lot adjacent to the casino and was amazed that it was almost full at 2:00 in the afternoon. In her naiveté, she thought gamblers came out at night, not during the middle of the day. Obviously, she was wrong.

She went to the information desk in the casino and got directions to where the private high stakes poker room was located. A few minutes later she stood in front of the doors to the room and introduced herself to the guard. She knew that entry into the room was only allowed at midnight, so she spent some time taking notes and pictures with her phone. Feeling much better about the upcoming appraisal, she decided to go into the coffee shop and have her favorite, a macchiato containing one shot of espresso with a little steamed milk. The frothy mixture was a perfect late afternoon drink.

After Marty got her drink, she looked around for a place to sit.

The coffee shop was completely full with every booth and table occupied. Again, she was surprised at the number of people who were in the casino building.

As she walked around, looking for someone about to leave, she noticed a beautiful little dog sitting quietly next to her owner's feet. She stopped at the woman's table and said, "That's a beautiful dog. Do you mind if I pet her?"

"Oh no, Miss Olive loves to be petted. Feel free to," the woman said, smiling and obviously happy that someone had noticed her dog.

Marty put her hand down so the dog could smell it. After a moment, Miss Olive licked her hand and only then did Marty pet her. "What a sweet girl you are," Marty said. She looked at the woman and said, "I'm a dog lover and I have a white boxer and a black Lab, but I'm unfamiliar with this breed. What is she?"

"She's an Italian Greyhound."

"I know nothing about the breed, but she's a beauty," Marty said, setting her drink down on the table and continuing to pet Miss Olive.

"Since there aren't any tables available, and there's an extra chair at my table, you're welcome to join me. My name is Marie Lewis."

"Thanks, I'll take you up on that, Marie. I'm Marty Morgan and I've always wanted to have a dog that I could take with me in my purse. Your dog's small enough, I'm sure you can do that. I'd love to know more about the breed."

"Yes, I take her with me wherever I go. She's petite and often this breed is referred to as an 'I.G.' or 'Iggy' because of being an Italian Greyhound. The breed is a sight hound type of dog, but she's a little special," the woman said as she took a sip from her coffee cup.

"Special in what way?"

"She senses things about people. You passed her test, but I've seen her stiffen up when certain people are around. Several times I've found out later that they were abusers or had committed crimes. I remember one time I was having my car washed, and I was sitting at one of the outside tables waiting for the car to be finished. Miss Olive was sitting next to me, completely stiff and as close to me as she could get.

"I had no idea what was going on as this was the first time she'd ever done anything like that. A few days later the car wash was on the news because the police had raided it and found a number of wanted criminals working there."

"Wow, I'm sure it gets your attention when she does that," Marty said.

"Yes. She's a registered therapy dog, but you probably don't want to hear that story."

"As a matter of fact, I'd love to. I'm becoming a believer in animals having special sensory powers. We're pretty convinced that my boxer, Patron, has some psychic abilities because of things that have happened in the past. How did you happen to get Miss Olive?"

"My sister saw something on Facebook about her. At the time I was homebound recovering from a car accident that required numerous surgeries and years of physical rehabilitation. I couldn't drive and had many mobility issues.

"I looked into adopting her, but there were a number of people who also wanted her. My husband and I arranged for the rescue rep to come to our home so we could be vetted. She put Miss Olive in my arms to see if she'd be comfortable with me. She fell asleep and snuggled into me. That was four years ago, and we've never been apart since.

"My doctor called her my miracle therapy dog. Without her, I'd probably still be in a wheelchair. Now, we own a condominium here at the casino and I even play poker occasionally at the private high roller's table. My husband's not much of a gambler, but I enjoy it.

"I got a big settlement from the automobile accident, so I decided what's money for if you can't have some fun with it? Although I have to admit after the woman in the condominium next to me got drunk and passed out right next to her front door, I've been second-guessing my decision to buy here."

"That sounds horrible. What happened?"

"I don't really know. She's an actress who used to be really popular, but I heard she got a bad facelift and work in Hollywood dried up for her. She moved here, actually right next to me, and I often see her at the high stakes poker table when I'm there. I've never seen her drink when she plays, so maybe she goes home and hits the bottle."

"Is she any good? It seems like you'd have to be pretty good if you were willing to play in the high rollers private room."

"Yes, I'd say she's good. I've seen her win from time to time, although, like everyone else, last night she lost to West Virginia. Come to think of it, I believe she bet more than she usually does, and she must have lost it all, which is probably why she got drunk."

"She passed out near her front door? She's lucky you found her."

"I don't know what she was thinking, although in her state, probably not much. And yes, she is lucky. The front doors to our condos are close together. I went to our door to make sure it was locked, and while I was there, I heard a commotion. I opened it and saw Joannie standing in front of the open front door of her condo. She was swaying back and forth and mumbling to herself. I asked her if she was all right and she said she'd had too much to drink. Then she slumped down onto the floor."

"What did you do?"

"I called my husband who'd been watching some old movie on TV. He usually waits up for me when I play. Anyway, we went over there and got her inside and in her bed. All her vital signs seemed to be fine, so we left her, but I'm sure she's not feeling very good today." She laughed. "Actually, it was already today when we left her about five this morning. It will be interesting to see what she has to say to me the next time I see her."

"I'd imagine whatever the conversation is it would start with an apology. I have a sister who has psychic abilities, and I can just imagine what she'd say about you and me having this conversation."

"Why is that?" Marie asked.

"Because it's such a coincidence. I'm an antique and art appraiser and I've been hired to appraise the Native American artifacts in the high rollers room here at the casino. I mean what are the chances of us having this conversation, and I'm going to be there tonight? Oh well, it is what it is. Have you ever noticed the Native American artifacts in the room?"

"I hate to admit it, but only in passing. I'm afraid when I'm gambling, I'm pretty oblivious to everything but what's happening on the table and in my hand."

"That's what I was told when I questioned having to appraise those items while a high stakes poker game was underway. Guess you're not alone," Marty said.

"No, I'm sure I'm not. The only thing that gets my attention is Miss Olive. The last two times I've played, she's been doing the freeze up thing. I don't know what that was all about. Maybe it was because I couldn't get a decent hand, and she was angry at the men who were winning."

"That would be interesting. A dog who only wanted her owner to win," Marty said with a laugh.

"Actually, it was a little more than that," Marie said. "I think Miss Olive may have felt something was wrong with the way the men were winning."

"In what way?"

"Well, a few nights ago there was an Asian man who couldn't lose. I mean he won practically every hand. I quit when I was down $25,000. That's the most I allow myself to lose. If and when that happens, and it doesn't happen very often, I leave the table. The night he was winning Miss Olive was not happy.

"Interestingly enough, the same thing happened last night. A man, I think he said he was from West Virginia, won most of the hands he was dealt. I hit my limit and left. Again, Miss Olive was not happy.

"As a matter of fact, I just saw someone in the hallway who was at the poker table last night. He told me he saw a tweet where a man who was a gambler had been murdered in his room here at the hotel that's attached to the casino. Apparently it happened right after he'd been playing here last night at the high stakes poker table. He said the casino was trying to keep it quiet because there was talk it was related to his big winnings."

"Oh my gosh. My husband's a detective with the Palm Springs Police Department and he was called into work early this morning on a homicide. I wonder if that was it?"

"I don't know, but it sounds pretty coincidental," Marie said. "And given that, what is he going to think about you conducting an appraisal in the middle of the night at the casino where someone was murdered? And the person who was murdered had played poker the night before in the very room where you're going to be appraising things?"

"To be honest, Marie, I don't think he's going to be all that thrilled about it. Hopefully, the fact that there are going to be guards there will make him comfortable with it."

"Well, when you talk to him tell him that the guards are very good. They patrol the room constantly. I've never even seen them leave the room to go to the bathroom. There is only one exit and that's through the main doors where two more guards are stationed when there's a game being played. I think you'll be perfectly safe."

"Thanks. If you're there tonight, I'll give you a wave."

"Well, I just might be. Maybe my luck has changed because of his death, although if the Asian man is there, I still may be a loser. And so saying, I need to take Miss Olive out for a little walk. I've really enjoyed talking to you, Marty, and I hope to see you again. Here's my card if you ever want to share a table again," she said with a laugh.

"Thanks, and here's mine. Yes, I'd love to share a table with you. Thanks for telling me about Miss Olive."

Marty knelt down and patted the little dog on her head. "Goodbye, Miss Olive. Take good care of your owner."

CHAPTER SEVEN

After Marty left the casino, she drove out of Palm Springs towards her home in High Desert, a small community located about thirty minutes north of Palm Springs. As she was driving home, she was debating with herself how she was going to tell Jeff about her midnight appraisal. It was a given he was not going to be happy about it, particularly when more than likely he was investigating the murder of a man who had played poker at the casino last night.

Finally admitting to herself that there was simply no way to sugarcoat it, she decided she'd tell him the truth when the opportunity arose and try not to make a big deal out of it. Of course, with Patron and Laura there, that would probably be easier said than done, given their psychic abilities and especially their sense of things that will occur in the future.

She parked her car in the driveway of the four-home compound she and Jeff shared with her sister, Laura, Laura's significant other and a world renown artist, Les, and John, the owner of the Red Pony Food Truck and Catering Company.

Every evening they shared dinner and the events of the day at the large table in the courtyard which was surrounded by their homes, joined most nights by Max, John's assistant. John used them nightly, unless he had a catering job, as guinea pigs for recipes he was trying out. Considering he was one of the best chefs in the Palm Springs area, and that's saying a lot, dinners in the courtyard were eagerly looked forward to by each of them.

The courtyard was magical, thanks to the efforts of Laura, the owner of the homes that made up the compound. Not only did she have a green thumb, she loved twinkly lights. The courtyard was like a rain forest with its exotic plants, and every branch of the large tree in the middle of it was covered with tiny twinkling lights.

When she walked through the gate, she was greeted by Patron and Duke, who always waited there for her to return home. After petting them, she waved to the compound residents and Max, John's assistant, as they sat at the table, enjoying a glass of wine.

"Hi guys. Give me a minute to walk the dogs and put my stuff away and then I'll join you," she said.

"Take your time," John responded. "I'll have a glass of wine waiting for you."

"Think I'll pass tonight, John. Thanks, anyway," she said as she walked into the desert with the two dogs.

As soon as she'd closed the gate, John looked at Jeff and said, "What's wrong with Marty? She never turns down a glass of wine at the end of the day."

Jeff looked at him and said, "Honestly? I have no idea. Maybe she's not feeling well."

"Don't think that's it," Laura said enigmatically.

"Think she's got a bun in the oven?" Max asked with a roguish smile.

"No, she is definitely not pregnant, and you can take that to the bank," Jeff said almost angrily, as if he had to defend Marty.

"Hey man, jes' sayin'," Max said, spreading his hands as if in defeat.

"No, she isn't pregnant and it's absolutely nothing earth-shattering like that," Laura said as she took a sip of her wine.

"I'm assuming you know what it is, Laura. Would I be right?" Jeff asked.

"This is Marty's business, not mine. When she's ready, she'll tell you."

"Okay, I guess that's as much as I'm going to get out of you. John, what's for dinner?"

"I was able to get some salmon from a friend of mine, but not enough to serve at the Pony, so thought we'd have it tonight. It's baked with mayonnaise spread on top and is super moist. That plus some bacon and cheese jalapeno poppers, and for dessert, a Heath Bar cake. Think you'll like it. I'll wait 'til Marty joins us, then I'll put the salmon and the poppers in the oven. I've already made the salad and the dessert, so it'll be easy."

"Sounds wonderful, John. As usual, you've outdone yourself. And since Heath Bars are my go-to sinful snack, you can just set aside a good portion of the cake for me," Les said with a smile.

"Trust me, there's nothing a chef likes better than having to serve a bunch of people who enjoy his food. I'm just glad that no persnickety eaters live here at the compound."

A few minutes later Marty returned from walking the dogs and joined the group at the table. All eyes were on her when she sat down.

"What? Why is everybody looking at me?" she asked.

"We're waiting to see why you don't want a glass of wine tonight. You always have some when we get together for dinner," John said.

She looked at Jeff who was looking at her very closely. "Yes, Marty, I'd like to know as well. Are you sick? If you are, you probably need to skip dinner and go to bed."

"No, I'm fine." She glanced at Laura whose face told her nothing. She took a deep breath and said, "I have an appraisal later on tonight, so I need a really clear head."

Jeff was the first to speak. "Marty, you never told me anything about an appraisal tonight. To my knowledge, you've never done an appraisal at night. What's up with that and why can't you do it during the day?"

Marty was quiet for several moments, but from the way she was twisting her hands, it was very apparent that she was nervous. "Well, you left really early this morning. Dick Costner, you know, Laura's boss at the insurance company, called me this morning about an appraisal."

"An appraisal that takes place at night," Jeff said in a very quiet voice. "Please tell me more about this appraisal. Where is it and when are you going?"

"Well, it's in a very public area. I'll be appraising some of the best artifacts the owners have."

"Marty, if you were a witness testifying at a trial, I would tell you to just answer the question. Let me remind you, I asked you where the appraisal was and when you were going to it. Please answer me."

No one spoke or moved as everyone waited for Marty's answer. It was very apparent to all of them that Jeff was not happy about the appraisal, and that might be putting it mildly.

"It's really quite an honor," she started to say, but was interrupted by Jeff.

"Marty, I'm losing my patience. I'm not going to ask you again. Tell me what I asked you."

"Okay, and I knew you'd feel this way. I'm appraising artifacts in the high rollers poker room at the casino. The only time the room is open to the public is from midnight to 4:00 a.m., so that's when they want me there," she said quickly.

Jeff was very quiet and then he said, "I'm hoping I misunderstood something you said. You're going to the casino in the middle of Palm Springs at midnight to do an appraisal. Is that right?"

"Yes, and I'm honored I was chosen to do it. Dick gave them my credentials as well as the credentials of some other appraisers, and I was the one they chose," she said defiantly.

"Would it be too much to ask why you can't conduct the appraisal during normal business hours?"

"Of course not. The artifacts in that room come from the tribe as well as some they took in trade over the years. It's thought to be one of the best Native American collections in existence."

"Marty, you're not answering my question."

"I was getting there. The room has a guard 24/7 and during the time it's open, it has three guards inside and two outside in front of the doors. Dick told me they felt it would be safer for me to be there with three guards. And Jeff, one of them is assigned exclusively to me. He'll meet me at my car when I get there, stay by my side during the appraisal, and walk me to my car when I'm finished for the night."

"And can you see that I'm jumping for joy over that tidbit? Does the word cheap mean anything to you?" Jeff asked.

"What do you mean?"

"The tribe, which is one of the wealthiest in the United States and owns half the land in Palm Springs, can't afford to have three guards with you during the day when things like this are normally done?" he said sarcastically.

"I asked about that, but I was told they were concerned about something happening to the artifacts if the room was open at another time."

"In other words, they care more about the artifacts than they do you."

"That's not fair, Jeff. It's a wonderful opportunity for me, and I'll be perfectly safe."

"Marty, there's a lot more to this than you know," Jeff said ominously.

"Jeff, sorry to interrupt, but I saw a little blurb on the early news this afternoon about some guy being murdered who was a high roller gambler. Said he was murdered in his room at the casino hotel. Is that part of your 'lot more'?" John asked.

"Yes, a man was murdered in his room at the casino about 4:30 this morning. What has not been released is that he was at the poker game in the high rollers private room last night. He won to the tune of $600,000. The thinking is he was murdered either for his winnings or because he won so big two nights in a row. However, we're having a problem with the motive being for his winnings, because his winnings were still on him."

Jeff turned to Marty. "In case you can't connect the dots, that means that you will be conducting your appraisal in the same room where the possible murderer may be playing poker tonight."

Marty turned white. "Well, with the guards there, I'm sure I'll be safe. You could always come with me if you're worried about my safety."

"I could, but in this case I can't because we've narrowed down the possible suspects to several people who often play high stakes poker at the casino. I don't want anyone to think they're a suspect, and there's a good chance someone would ID me. If you go, you'll have to go by yourself, but I'm sure you'll do the sensible thing and decide not to do this appraisal."

Marty was quiet for several moments and then said, "Jeff, I know you're worried about my safety, and I understand that. But look back on all the times I've been involved in helping you with a case when a crime has been committed. This isn't the first time I've been around possible suspects. And I won't even be interacting with them. Honest, I'll be fine."

"I take it from that statement that you're going to do the appraisal."

"Yes, I've worked too hard to build my business and the insurance company is one of my best clients. I can't just flake on them. As a matter of fact, I can help. Tell me who the suspects are, and I'll see if I can detect something."

"Jeff, Marty, before you go any further, I need to serve dinner. It's ready and there's nothing worse than ruining a good piece of salmon. Max and I will be back in just a minute with dinner."

CHAPTER EIGHT

"Oh, John, you really have a magic touch in the kitchen. I could eat at a different five-star restaurant every night and not eat as well as we eat here. Thank you so much," Les said.

Everyone had talked animatedly during dinner, trying to avoid the topic of the two-ton elephant in the room, Marty's appraisal at the casino later that night. After they'd all finished eating the Heath Bar cake, with kudos to the chef, Marty brought the subject up.

"Okay, Jeff, might as well get back to the subject of the appraisal and murder. I am going to do the appraisal. I think the sensible thing for you to do would be to tell me something about the possible suspects and then I can tell you if I notice anything."

He was quiet for several moments and then he said, "All right Marty, we'll play it your way. I'm not happy about your decision, but I'll accept it. Guess I don't have a choice. Since the victim gambled for his living, we've pretty much narrowed the list of possible suspects to the members of the gambling community. And since he was murdered at the casino here in Palm Springs, naturally we're focusing our attention there."

"Do you think he was killed because he'd been winning big?" Marty asked.

"Why do I think you know something I don't know?" Jeff asked.

"I went to the casino today to scope out what I was going to be appraising tonight. I knew I couldn't get into the room, so I stood outside, told the guard who I was, and took a lot of notes and photos."

"Did the guard tell you about the murder?" Jeff asked.

"No. After I finished taking notes and photos, I went to the coffee shop and had an interesting conversation with a woman there. Here's what she had to say." Marty told him about the conversation she'd had with Marie.

"Nice we have someone that's not a suspect who plays poker in the high rollers private room. That could be very important. Do you have any way of getting in touch with her?"

"Yes, we exchanged cards."

"Keep her card. I don't know when and how we might need her, but it's nice to know there's someone kind of on our side. Okay, the first suspect is an aging actress who came to the desert to retire, owns a condominium at the casino, and most nights plays poker in the high rollers private card room."

"Jeff, I think you can cross her off the list."

"Why? How could you possibly know anything about her?"

"Coincidence, pure and simple and I know how much you hate the word. Marie, the woman that I talked to in the coffee shop lives next door to Joannie Lambert. Marie heard a commotion when she was making sure her door was locked last night, actually around 4:30 this morning and found Joannie standing in her doorway, weaving, and obviously drunk.

"She passed out and Marie and her husband put her to bed, after making sure she was alright. From what Marie told me, she was in no shape to do anything to anyone."

"Well, that's interesting. No, from the way the man was murdered, it was too sophisticated for someone who was drunk to do it."

"How was he murdered, Jeff? The blurb I saw on the news didn't mention it," Les asked.

"That's because we're keeping it from the public at this time. It was very unusual. Someone put a fentanyl patch in his hand with enough of the opioid in it to kill him. We can only surmise that he answered the door and whoever it was, put their hand out to shake his, and transferred the fentanyl to the victim."

"Jeff, if he opened the door, that would almost indicate that he knew them, right?" Marty asked.

"We're proceeding under that assumption, and that's why we're primarily looking at the people he was playing poker with. He moves around so much it's unlikely that it was someone he happened to know in Palm Springs. And as I said, what really has our attention is that we found a $600,000 check in his possession. That tells us he was probably not murdered for his money, but instead definitely points to someone killing him so he couldn't gamble anymore and win continuously, as he has been."

"Is there talk that he was using some system for cheating?" Laura asked.

"None. I had one of my men pull up everything he could find out about the man. He gave an interview last year to a Midwest newspaper. I found it very interesting and probably up your alley, Laura."

"How so?" she asked.

"The interviewer asked him how he won so consistently. By the way, it's been pretty well documented that he changed casinos every three to four days. Casinos asked him not to come back, because they thought he must be using some system that was unacceptable to them."

"And from what you're saying, I'm gathering he didn't," Laura said.

"Not that he'd admit. Here's the interesting part. He told the interviewer that his mind was like a computer. He had what is called an eidetic memory and was able to recall every card that had been played. He also said it was like there was a computer in his brain that told him what the odds were of any card being dealt. He said he'd never found a psychiatrist, psychologist, or anyone else, who had any experience with someone who was born with that type of a mind."

"What do you make of it, Jeff?" Marty asked.

"I don't know. At this point there's absolutely no evidence that he was cheating."

"Okay, Jeff. Can you stop just long enough for me to bring out some coffee? I want to hear about the rest of the suspects, but I could use a cup. Anyone else join me?"

It was unanimous. Everyone became quiet while John and Max got the coffee.

CHAPTER NINE

When the coffee had been poured and everyone had added cream or sugar, if that was their preference, John said, "Okay, Jeff. Please continue. But I have a question, and I'd bet somebody else has the same question. From time to time, I know some of the casinos in the area have had problems with their dealers cheating. Any hint of that being true here?"

"No. I talked to some of the men who supervise that room and the dealers. I even talked to the pit boss. He said there was absolutely nothing that would indicate one of their dealers was cheating. Lance played there two nights, the second being the night he was murdered. After he won big on the first night, that table was under intense scrutiny, but they couldn't find anything that would implicate the dealer."

"What if he was so good it wasn't apparent?" Les asked.

"Could happen I suppose, and they even told me that, however, it's extremely doubtful. The one thing I did find interesting is that several days earlier an Asian man had won big for several nights, but once Lance arrived, the Asian man never won again."

"What does that tell you?" Laura asked.

"If it were my casino, I'd be looking closely at the table. Having two big winners so close together is very suspicious. I looked up the information on the Asian man and all I could find was several articles about him being from a wealthy family living in China. Evidently he and his wife like to come to the United States and gamble from time to time."

"His wife gambles as well?" Marty asked.

"No. What I meant was he and his wife come to the U.S. and he gambles. I found no record of her gambling anywhere."

"Jeff, two thoughts," Marty said. "First, the Asian man could have murdered Lance because he brought his winning streak to a close. Secondly, wouldn't it be unusual for a dealer to cheat for two men? I mean, first there was the Asian man, and then there was Lance. Seems like that would really be far-fetched, a crooked dealer working for two different men."

"Yes, I agree, which is why the dealer is very low on my suspect list. The last suspect that's on my list, and I'm well aware there could be others, is a man named Mark Cohen. He's quite wealthy and travels around the United States going to casinos where there are high stakes poker games. He wins big and like Lance, is usually asked to leave after a few days."

"It sounds like he's just a wealthy man who likes to gamble. Why would he be on your list, Jeff?" Les asked.

"He's used to winning. In the research we did today, it seems Mark and Lance were well-known to one another and had often played together with Lance always winning. Last night was Mark's first night at the casino here in Palm Springs. He played and he lost to Lance. I'm wondering if he snapped because of it."

"That's an interesting theory," Les said. "Marty, I'd be curious to know whether or not he plays tonight and if so, whether he wins."

"Speaking of which, I need to change clothes and leave. I don't want to be late for the appraisal." She turned to Jeff and said, "While

I'm there I'll glance over to see who's playing and who's winning. I wouldn't have a clue how to go about telling if someone is cheating. I'll leave that up to the guys who are watching the action that goes on in the private poker room. See you all tomorrow, and I don't mean in the morning. I'll probably sleep most of the day."

Jeff stood up and walked to the house with her. When they got inside, he pulled her close and said, "Marty, I really am concerned about your safety. There's a very good chance that you're going to be in a room with a murderer. Please be careful."

"I will, I promise, but think about it, Jeff. There is no reason for those people to have any interest in me. I'll just be a person in the background, taking pictures and making notes, but I will keep an eye out and see if I notice anything."

"All right. And I agree that if there is something going on with the dealer, it would probably be far beyond your card-playing ability to pick up. Just promise me one thing."

"What's that?"

"If you sense anything is dangerous, wrong, or a threat, you'll leave and call me immediately. Tell them you're sick or something. Promise?"

"Pinky swear," she said as she stood on her tiptoes and kissed him. "I love you. See you in a few hours."

"Trust me, I'll be waiting for you."

CHAPTER TEN

Marty got in her car, made sure her doors were locked, and began the half-hour drive to Palm Springs. When she got to the casino, she went to valet parking, where Dick had told her to park, and that he would call and give her name to the valet stand. He also said the casino would provide a guard to walk her to the high rollers private card room.

The valet placed a call and a moment later, a guard walked out of the casino and over to her car. "Ms. Morgan, my name's Jerome, and I'll be your personal guard while you're here at the casino conducting your appraisal."

"Nice meeting you, Jerome. I appreciate your help. I just need to get a few items out of my trunk for my appraisal."

"Not a problem," he said.

She opened the trunk of her car and took out her camera and her briefcase, which Jerome took from her. When they walked into the casino, she paused, looking at a sea of humanity playing machines, walking to restaurants, carrying drinks, and all with a backdrop of the sound of slot machines. It was enough to give her a headache.

She and Jerome walked down the hall to where the high rollers poker room was located. She saw a guard standing in front of the glass doors as they approached. Jerome introduced her to the guard, who let them into the room. Dick had told her that he'd arranged for her to be let into the room ten minutes before it would open for the games at midnight, the same time the dealers and the guards were let into the room.

His contact at the casino had felt it would be good for Marty to get set up before the games began. Dick's contact had told him that the less intrusions on the games, the better.

Marty and Jerome proceeded to the back of the room where the artifacts were displayed. Some were hanging on brackets attached to the wall and others were contained in glass display cases. Jerome told her he'd be happy to take the pieces off of the wall for her and when she was finished, he'd put them back. That would give her an opportunity to personally examine each item, something that was necessary if she was going to do a thorough appraisal that could stand up in a dispute if one arose.

She walked over to the back corner of the room and took out her tape measure and a pad of paper. Although she preferred to dictate her appraisals, Dick had told her that the card room was very, very quiet and they didn't want her making any unusual sounds, which her dictation would do. Therefore, she had to go back to conducting an appraisal much as she had when she'd first started appraising years ago, by writing down information and data on a pad of paper.

She unsnapped her camera case and put her camera on a long table that had been provided for her. There was a fresh pitcher of water and a glass on it. When she was finished, she heard noises and saw twenty-one players being admitted into the room and sitting seven to a table.

Marty turned back to the artifacts she'd be appraising and on the far end of the glass exhibit case she saw a neatly prepared information sheet about the exhibit. She walked over to it, read it, gasped, and then smiled broadly.

The exhibit had been curated by her good friend, Carl Mitchell, who owned The Olde Antique Shoppe in downtown Palm Springs. Not only was Carl her friend, she'd used him numerous times to appraise items that were out of her areas of expertise. Unfortunately, several of them had involved people who had been murdered.

Carl had never forgotten two of the appraisals, particularly the one in which Marty's sister, Laura, who was helping her with it, had a psychic sense that the missing diamond ring they were looking for was in a Styrofoam wig stand. She'd walked into the room with a large kitchen knife, terrorizing Carl, and whacked the wig stand in half. The ring was hidden inside it.

On another appraisal, Patron, Marty's white boxer that Laura was certain had psychic abilities, was keeping Carl company in the garage while he was appraising items. When he picked up an unusual looking knife, Patron became frantic and again, Carl was terrified. The knife later proved to be seminal in solving the murder that had taken place at the home where the appraisal was being conducted.

After that Carl had promised himself and Marty that he would never do an appraisal with Marty if either Laura or Patron was involved. He had a healthy respect and liking for each of them, but not enough to be involved with them when their psychic senses were in full-blown action

Aside from his antique shop and his appraising, Carl might best be known for his ability to know a little bit about everything that was going on in the Palm Springs area. The art and antiques in his shop were excellent, but the gossip was even better. Marty was fairly certain that half the people who went to his antique shop went there as much for the gossip as they did for the art and antiques.

Marty made a mental note to call him tomorrow and see what he knew about the casino and the murder. She walked the length of the glass display cases and saw that each item in the cabinets and those hanging on the wall had a card next to it giving the name of the item, where it came from, its approximate date, and any other information that was pertinent. She knew that was going to make this appraisal very, very easy to do.

She smiled at Jerome, the guard assigned to her, and quietly whispered that she'd like the first cabinet's glass doors opened, and he could start taking the items off of the walls so she could begin examining them.

While he was getting a beaded cradleboard down from its holder and putting it on the long table that had been brought in for her to use, she looked around. The card room was very quiet. Only the gamblers' voices were heard and then only saying something that dealt with the game that was underway.

She looked at the gamblers. There were two women, the rest being men. There were various ethnicities at each of the tables. Jeff had shown her photos of Diego, Mark, and John. She recognized Diego from his picture and that of Mark, who was playing at another table. Although there were several Asian men playing, John was not one of them. Diego and Mark were the only two in the room that Jeff had spoken of earlier.

She turned around and began to appraise the items in the collection beginning with the cradleboard. She'd have to ask Carl why he hadn't been chosen to do the appraisal. She imagined it was because of a possible conflict of interest. If a loss occurred and Carl had sold the items to the casino, and then later appraised them, that could become a problem. Carl had a number of excellent Native American artifacts in his shop, and she was certain that some of the items in the cases had been sold to the casino by Carl.

Halfway through the four-hour time period she'd been allotted, she told the guard she needed to use the ladies room. He closed and locked the display cabinet she was working on and escorted her out of the room and down the hall to the ladies room. When she walked out, he was waiting for her and escorted her back to the private cardroom.

She noticed about ten people standing in a line in front of the high rollers room. "Jerome, are those people waiting to get in?"

"Yes, there's only room for twenty-one people at the tables. Some people play for a couple of hands to see how their luck is and then if it's not good, they leave. There's always someone waiting to replace them. There was a line when we came in earlier, but you probably didn't notice it."

When they were back in the card room and Jerome was unlocking one of the glass doors on a display cabinet, she said, "Jerome, does that big pile of chips in front of that man over at the table on the end mean he's winning big?"

"Sure does. And you probably didn't notice, but there's been a steady stream of people sitting at that table for a couple of hands and then leaving. When someone has a pile of chips that big, it's always a gamble on whether they're just having a phenomenal night or they're going to crash and burn. All the people playing at that table right now are gambling, literally, that he's going to crash."

"How much money do those chips represent right now?" Marty asked.

"I'd say about half a million dollars. There's a reason they call this room the high rollers room. You're looking at it. And funny thing about the guy with all the chips. Last night he lost every hand to that guy you probably read about in the paper, the guy who was murdered in his hotel room here at the casino."

"Yes, I heard about it. Did he come here much?"

"I'd never seen him before he showed up a couple of nights ago. He took almost every hand while he was playing. I could see the pit boss trying to figure out if he was cheating or doing something, but evidently not, because he let the guy keep playing. It was pretty unusual, though."

"Does that happen very often?"

"Once in a while someone, as I said earlier, gets on a hot streak. It happens. The only other guy I've seen win three nights in a row was an Asian man, but he lost to the guy who died. He's not here tonight.

Maybe he's at another casino, although we have the highest limit poker tables in the Palm Springs area. Dunno' what happened to him."

"Okay, thanks. Time for me to get back to business."

Marty spent the remaining time engrossed in her work. At 3:45 Jerome said, "That should be your last piece, Ms. Morgan. I want to lock the cases and make sure everything's where it should be. You can do the rest tomorrow night."

"Thanks, Jerome. I had no idea it was that late. I really appreciate all your help."

"Not a problem. Why don't you give me your valet ticket? I'll text the valet stand and make sure your car will be at the front door when we get there. I'll walk you to it."

"You don't have to do that. I can walk there by myself."

"Ms. Morgan. Word came down from on high that your husband is a detective with the Palm Springs Police Department. I was told to take care of you from the moment you parked your car until the moment you got back in it. If I don't do that, I'll probably be fired, and you wouldn't want to be responsible for that, would you?"

"No, sir," Marty said with a laugh as they walked out of the room. "Jerome, I do have one last question."

"Shoot," he said as they walked through the crowded casino.

"What's up with the riotous carpeting? I mean its bright colors and patterns are unlike any I've ever seen. Makes a statement, but I'm not sure of just what."

"I agree. Here's what I was told when I asked that same question when I started working here. Supposedly a lot of psychological testing has been done on what makes people gamble. For instance, you'll never see a clock or an open window in a casino, because if gamblers see that it's dawn or some other relation to time, they stop gambling. There should be no sense of time in a casino."

"Okay, I can understand that, but what about the carpeting?"

"Kind of the same theory as fast food restaurants. The brighter the colors the more the people eat, and here, the more they gamble. Kind of jacks up the senses, if you will."

"Amazing, simply amazing. And I assume this carries through to every little detail, even the color of the cards."

"That's right. Loud sounds, bright colors, and no sense of time make people spend more. Good, there's your car."

He walked her over to it and the valet opened the driver's door for Marty. She handed him a tip, and said, "See you tomorrow night, Jerome. Thanks for doing such a great job for me."

"My pleasure, Ms. Morgan. I enjoyed it. I'll be here when you return tomorrow."

CHAPTER ELEVEN

Although the casino was still amazingly busy at 4:00 a.m. in the morning, the rest of Palm Springs was not. Marty had the roads to herself on the drive back to the compound. Between the appraisal and the conversations with Marie and Jeff, her mind was spinning.

I'd rather not get into it again with Jeff. Hopefully he'll be sleeping, and I won't have to talk to him until tonight, she thought. *Think it would be better for both of us.*

She turned into the compound's driveway and saw that a light was on in her house. *Well, so much for that. Guess I'm going to have to face the music, like it or not.*

She got her appraisal equipment out of her car, opened the gate, and realized it was the first time she'd ever come home that Duke and Patron weren't waiting at the gate for her.

When she opened the door the smell of coffee hit her and she heard Jeff say, "Good early morning to you. I decided to get up early and go to work, but the main reason I got up early is that I wanted to see you before I left." He walked over to her and hugged her. "How did it go?"

"It was different from any appraisal I've ever done, that's for sure. Let me get some water, and I'll tell you all about it. I need to get some sleep and coffee would definitely not help."

She spent the next half hour telling him about the appraisal, the casino, and the players in the high rollers card room.

"Marty, you're sure you didn't see John Chen? With Lance dead and John's earlier wins in the high rollers card room, I thought for sure he'd be there tonight," Jeff said

"No, I have a pretty good memory for visuals. That's one of the things a good appraiser has to have and no, he definitely was not playing tonight."

"Well, I need to follow up on that first thing today. I know he's been staying in a room at the casino hotel. Maybe he decided to go elsewhere, but still, I'm surprised. And you said that the man named Mark was winning big."

"Very big, according to the guard, Jerome. He also told me that Mark had lost to Lance the last two nights. Jerome said he was surprised that Mark hadn't left town when it was clear that Lance was on a roll."

"I agree with him. I would think most people would. I find that rather strange. Was he sitting at the table where Diego was the dealer?"

"No, but I did look at Diego's table from time to time when he was dealing."

"I'm sure I know the answer to this, Marty, but did you notice Diego doing anything strange? Did anything seem off to you?"

"No, not at all, but then I don't know enough about gambling or poker to know if something was off."

"Yeah, that's what I figured." He looked at the kitchen clock and said, "Time for me to leave and for you to get some sleep. I need to find out what happened to Chen and sometime today I should get the coroner's report."

"I absolutely need to get some sleep. Since Carl was responsible for the exhibit and the legends of the pieces I'm appraising, I want to go into Palm Springs for a little while this afternoon and talk to him. I hate making two trips there the same day, but I'd really prefer to talk to Carl in person."

"Well, while you're there, see what the latest gossip in town is. Heck, he might even know something about the murder, as close to the ground as his ear is. Go get some sleep. I'll feed the dogs and walk them. See you tonight. And Marty, I do love you. I hope you know the only reason I sometimes get a little angry is because I'm so worried about your safety."

"I know, Jeff, and I'm glad you do care that much for me, but now that I have Jerome watching over me, and by the way, he's armed with a gun, I'll be just fine. Loves," she said as she walked into the bedroom and collapsed on the bed. Moments later she was sound asleep.

CHAPTER TWELVE

Marty rolled over and looked at the clock on her nightstand. It read 2:30. She'd slept solidly for 8 ½ hours. Even though she felt rested she thought that there was no way she could ever work a night shift and was very glad tonight was the last night of the appraisal.

She got out of bed and almost tripped over Patron and Duke, who were not used to their master sleeping during the day. They felt something was wrong and knew it was their obligation to protect her, but from what, they had no idea.

"Good afternoon, guys. I need coffee, a shower, and some food. Then I'll take you out. Deal?" She waited for an answer, but got none. "I'll take that as a yes," she said as she walked into the kitchen, the two dogs right behind her.

An hour later she was driving down the hill to Palm Springs. She'd called Carl to make sure he was in his shop and he assured her that he would be there waiting for her.

She pulled up in front of The Olde Antique Shoppe, which was practically an institution in Palm Springs, parked and walked through the door, the little bell above the door announcing her.

As soon as she stepped through the door, she was enveloped in a bear hug by the owner of the shop, Carl.

"Marty, it's so good to see you. I know you told me you wanted to talk to me about the appraisal you're doing at the casino, but first I have to show you some utter cuteness," Carl said as he led Marty back to his office

"Be very quiet," he whispered. "I just got her to sleep, but I want you to see the adorable little outfit Miss Simone's wearing. I'll open the door just a little, so you can see in. I keep a night light on for her so she won't get scared."

With that he opened the door just far enough for Marty to look into his office and at the little Maltipoo who was asleep on a very large pink satin dog pillow embroidered with sequins.

Marty looked at the dog, back at Carl, and then again at the dog, not quite believing what she was seeing. Miss Simone was wearing a pink silk bodysuit with white mink cuffs ending just above her paws.

"Carl, those cuffs look like real mink. Would I be right?"

"Yes, I just couldn't resist it when I saw that outfit online at a rather exclusive dog's clothing store where I like to shop. Isn't she just beautiful in it?"

"Carl, we're in Palm Springs, not Buffalo, New York. Don't you think she may get hot in that outfit?"

"Oh, Marty, don't be ridiculous. Of course I know where we live. That's why I keep the temperature set at 60 degrees in my office when she wears her fur outfits. It's not good for a dog to overheat you know, and I wouldn't want anything to happen to Miss S. She's my baby."

"I know that Carl, and she's adorable. I remember you telling me that you and she were going to dress alike. Are you still doing that?"

"Sometimes, but darling, there is no way I'm going to wear a pink silk bodysuit with white mink cuffs. Really, you surprise me. I mean, what would people think?"

Probably exactly what they're already thinking, Marty thought.

"I think that was a good call, Carl. Pink is definitely not your color."

"Oh, you are so silly," he said as he quietly closed the door. "But I think you'll have to agree with me. It's definitely Miss S's color."

"Yes, I totally agree," Marty said, thinking *I am so glad Jeff isn't with me to hear this conversation.* The image of Jeff with a dog in pink silk trimmed with mink was something that would never happen in a million years. Maybe a dog with a leather stud collar and a chain link leash, but Miss S's outfit, no way.

She remembered how Duke used to hate to go out in the desert. There was something about his feet on the desert floor that he completely resisted. For several months she had to plead, wheedle, and cajole to even get him off of the front walkway to commune with nature.

One day she'd been surfing the web, trying to find out the cause of his odd behavior and ran across a site that advertised booties for dogs who refused to walk on certain surfaces. She bought a pair of booties, but the only color they came in was pink.

The booties worked, but Jeff usually found one excuse or another as to why he couldn't take Duke out in the desert. She was pretty sure he was afraid it might hurt his tough detective image if anyone saw him walking a dog wearing pink booties.

When she and Jeff had been on their honeymoon in Hawaii, Les had taken it upon himself to break Duke of the bootie habit. When they returned, they were met with Les and Duke happily walking on the desert floor, Duke without his booties. When they asked him about it, Les had said it was kind of like housebreaking, you just had to be consistent and he had been. He told Marty and Jeff it was his wedding gift to them.

She smiled at the memory and then returned to the present. "As you know, I'm appraising the exhibit you curated at the casino. What can you tell me about it?"

"It should be a super easy appraisal for you. All you really need to do is take pictures. There's a legend next to each piece with the dimensions and pertinent information on it. The one thing you'll have to do is put the insurance replacement amounts on it, and based on the rarity of some of those items, you're going to have to use your best guess based on the auction or sale prices of similar items.

"It's kind of one of those things where nothing like it has been on the market so it's worth whatever you say. And who's going to argue with that?"

"Carl, did you sell the casino any of the items?"

"Yes, over a period of years I'd say I sold them about half of the items, but some of them were bought over twenty years ago. I'd be happy to email you the amount they bought the items from me for, but that's just a place to start. And a lot of the ones I didn't sell to them have been owned by the tribe for many, many years, again making a judgment on replacement cost very difficult."

"I kind of figured when you weren't doing the appraisal it was because you'd sold them some of the items and that gets into the grey area," Marty said.

"True. Dick, I think he's your sister's boss, called me about it when he saw my name on the exhibit. He told me he couldn't hire me because of the possible conflict of interest, and I suggested you. Dick said you were going to be his next call, because you always do such a good job for him."

"Well, that's nice to hear. The items really are fantastic."

"I know," he said almost in a whisper. "And the best part is that even though a murder has been associated with that high stakes card room, I don't have to get involved in it."

"That's true. Carl, you have the best network system in Palm Springs. What are you hearing about the murder?"

"Not much. The majority of my clients are residents of the Palm Springs area. The people who play in the high rollers room, with a few exceptions, often come from out of town. It's my understanding the professional gamblers pretty much follow a circuit. I know a couple of people who play there, but that's about it."

"Like who?"

"You know that old movie star, Joannie Lambert?"

"Sure, everyone knows her."

"Well, when her face lift went south, she recently moved to Palm Springs, bought one of the condos in the casino complex, and started playing high stakes poker there from time to time. She's bought a lot of things from me since she moved here. Matter of fact, we had an appointment scheduled for yesterday, but she called and had to cancel it."

"Did she say why?" Marty asked.

"Yes, evidently she'd been losing big the last couple of nights. She told me she lost one night to an Asian man and two nights to a West Virginia man. Said the next time she played it would be with someone from California. She said the reason she couldn't come to the shop was because she was too hung over."

"Is that a common occurrence with her?"

"No, I think she enjoys a cocktail now and then, but I've never heard of her overindulging. Joannie said she lost a lot of money two nights ago, and she had a couple of drinks when she got home. She said she remembers seeing her neighbor and then passing out. The next thing she remembers is waking up in her bed with a splitting headache and vowing never to drink vodka again."

"What did the neighbor have to do with it?"

"Joannie says she called the neighbor when she finally woke up and they confirmed they'd put her to bed," Carl said.

"I'd be pretty thankful for that neighbor."

"She was. I asked her if I'd know the neighbor and it turns out she's one of my best customers and a class act. Plus, she has the cutest little Italian Greyhound you've ever seen. Her dog's name is Miss Olive, and she just loves Miss S."

"Oh, I know her. I met her the other day at the casino coffee shop. Nice lady," Marty said.

"Not only is she nice, but I think her dog is kind of like Patron and your sister, you know, psychic."

"What makes you say that?"

"Oh, Marie always brings Miss Olive with her when she comes to the shop, and she's told me a number of things Miss Olive has done. I saw one in action."

"What was that?"

"Well, Marie and I were talking and there were a couple of customers in the store. Miss Olive was in Marie's purse with her head sticking out. She stiffened, which Marie had told me was a sign something bad was going on with someone. About that time a man hurried out the door and the chime went off. Then I heard Danielle yell, "Stop, or I'm calling the police."

"What happened?"

"She'd seen one of the men put a piece of silver in his shirt and then walk towards the door. Danielle was walking towards me to tell me about it when the man raced out the door."

"Did he come back?"

"Are you kidding? He hotfooted it down the street as fast as he could. I ran out of the shop, but he was nowhere in sight. Oh well, at least the silver piece is a write-off."

"And you think her dog sensed it?"

"No, I don't think her dog sensed it. I'd bet everything that Miss Olive knew the man was stealing something. I wish Miss S. had that ability, but she's not good for much besides love."

"Well, sometimes, that's enough."

"Agreed. Marty, great talking to you, as always, but the shop has filled up with customers, and I don't want Danielle to get overburdened. I'll send you what I have on the items you're appraising, and if I can do anything, let me know. And by the way, glad this appraisal doesn't have a murder involved in it."

Well, there may be, Marty thought. *But Carl doesn't need to know that.*

CHAPTER THIRTEEN

Marty looked at the dashboard clock on her car and realized she still had a little time before her friends would be meeting in the courtyard for dinner. She decided to stop in at the Hi-Lo Drugstore and leave off some photographs for Lucy to develop.

She walked into the store and was amazed to see several people gathered around Lucy. In all the times she'd been in the drugstore she'd seen one or two people at Lucy's counter, but that was about it. She walked over to the crowd and was greeted by Lucy.

"Hey, girlfriend, ya' sure picked the right day to come here. My ol' man decided to make Killer into a huntin' dog and durned if he didn't make the ol' man proud. Got him a coupla' birds first time out. Thought the ol' man was gonna' burst with pride. Ya' know how he is 'bout that animal, course I ain't much better."

Hunting had never been Marty's favorite sport, but when Lucy passed over the photographs of Killer and Lucy's ol' man, she had to agree they both looked as if they were bursting with pride. The people around her smiled, made supportive comments to Lucy, and then left to do whatever they'd come into the store to do.

"Whaddya think? Don't those photos jes' beat all?"

"Lucy, I can honestly say I don't think I've ever seen a dog and a man who looked any prouder than those two. Think your husband will take him hunting again?"

"I dunno'. He said all them snowflakes come down here to Palm Springs for the warm weather and a lot of 'em like to hunt. Says sometimes they jes' overrun everythin'. 'Tween you and me, I think he's jes' worried somethin'll happen to Killer."

"I think the people you are referring to are called 'snowbirders' Lucy, not 'snowflakes'. Anyway, he does love that dog, doesn't he?" Marty asked.

"Yeah. Matter-of-fact, if push came to shove, and he had to make a choice on whether he'd pick Killer or me, I think there's a good chance I'd be odd man out. Don't make me real happy, but I gotta say, I love Killer as much as he does. Who knows who I'd pick, given the same choice?"

"Well, let's hope it never comes to that," Marty said, as she took the memory card out of her digital camera so Lucy could develop the pictures she'd taken of the objects at the casino.

Lucy glanced at them and said, "Ya' must be doin' that room where the guy who was offed was gamblin'."

"What makes you say that?"

"Where else would it be? None of the other tribes around here got stuff like that. Anyway, the ol' man and I saw them things one time. We was at the casino hopin' to get rich, but didn't happen. Guess it never will on the penny slots. Oh well. Anyways, we took a break to stretch our legs cuz' five hours at the same machine jes' made my legs fall asleep. Had to be real careful I didn't fall down when I stood up."

"You sat at a penny slot machine for five hours?" Marty asked in disbelief.

"Yep, woulda' stayed there longer cuz' that sucker was way overdue to pay big, but the ol' man said we'd had enough. Anyway, we took us a little walk to look in that private card room where the gazillionaires play. Woo hoo! Loved the baskets. Wouldn't mind a coupla' of them to keep stuff in. Ya' know, like my make-up and stuff. They was real purty."

"Lucy, those baskets are easily worth many hundreds of dollars, maybe more. Not quite the thing for a make-up holder."

"Then what's somethin' good fer if you can't use it? Don't wanna' spend my hard-earned money on some little thing ya' jes' look at and say, 'Oh, ain't that nice?' Waste of money if ya' ask me."

As an antique and art appraiser, I hate to say it, but she might just be right, Marty thought.

"Well, a lot of things that are collected today were originally made to be used for something. Eventually people decided they should just be appreciated."

"Purty stupid, if ya' ask me. Okay, girlfriend, I can see ya' got that 'have to leave now look in yer' eye', but gotta' read ya' my sayin' of the day. Here goes, 'You never know how important you are to someone until they can't have you.' Jes' what I've been thinkin' lately and they spelled it out better than I could."

"Sorry, Lucy, but you've lost me," Marty said.

"Look at it this way. Maybe if somethin' happened to me, the ol' man would realize how important I am and he'd start kissin' me like he kisses Killer."

"Lucy, you know you've always been the most important thing in the world to your husband, but it says something very good about him that he has enough love in his heart to open it up for a dog and also have you in there."

Lucy looked at Marty with tears in her eyes. "Yeah, yer' probably right. Jes' sometimes I ferget. Girlfriend, ya' always know the right things to say. Thanks."

"Happy to be of help. I'll probably be in tomorrow. Tell your husband those are great photos."

"If he's still alive and ain't bursted with pride, I will," Lucy said.

CHAPTER FOURTEEN

John Chen walked out of the high rollers room after two hours of playing. It looked like the West Virginian was going to clean up again, just like he had the evening before, so there was no point in staying. He'd looked at Diego several times and Diego had almost imperceptibly moved his head from side to side, which indicated to John that the man wasn't using a system. He was just a phenomenally lucky gambler.

It was probably time to get the fentanyl Lily had set out for him and just do away with the man. He'd prefer it if Diego took care of it, but he couldn't afford to wait another night. As much as he hated the thought of taking a life, but according to Lily, and he had to agree with her, they couldn't wait any longer. If this kept on, John and the people Lily had recruited, would lose everything they'd won over the past few weeks.

His thoughts turned to Lily, and he wondered what she'd found out about her tests. If the outcome wasn't good, he planned on finding the best doctors he could for her. She meant the world to him, and he'd do whatever it took to make sure she was healed.

He walked down the hall towards the hotel/condo section of the casino where he and Lily were staying. He took his phone out of his pocket to see if she'd texted him. She had.

John, no matter what time you get this, come directly to the front of the casino. A driver by the name of Jing will be waiting for you. Don't bother returning to our room, I've packed everything. I chartered a plane to fly us to China immediately. I'm in the plane now. As you can guess, the doctor's report was not good. I will tell you all about it when I see you. Hurry, John, I have no time to waste, she'd texted.

John stopped in the hallway and read the text two more times. He knew the doctor's report had to be very, very bad for Lily to leave after all the work she'd done with the people she'd hired to watch Diego's false shuffle and make it profitable. When the impact of the text hit him, he started running through the casino towards the front door.

He raced through the casino doors and spotted a black town car with an Asian man standing next to it. John ran over to it. "Are you Jing?" he asked the man who was already opening the door for him.

"Yes, Mr. Chen. Your wife is waiting for you at the airport. We'll be there shortly."

*****

Jeff did paperwork while he waited for the rest of his staff to come in that morning. When he noticed that the room had filled up, he called one of his deputies. "Mac, would you come into my office for a moment? I have something I want you to look into."

A few moments later there was a knock on the door. "Come in," Jeff said as a tall man with a ponytail and an earring walked into his office. He was wearing a Snoop Dogg t-shirt with faded jeans that were torn at the knees. As he looked at him, Jeff thought once again that no one would ever think Mac Stewart was a detective with the Palm Springs Police Department. What they wouldn't know was that he was one of the best undercover detectives the department had.

"Sir, what can I do for you?" Mac asked.

"It concerns a man named John Chen. He's been gambling for

several nights in the high rollers room at the casino here in town. He wasn't in the room for two hours last night, and I'd like to know why. I don't have much to go by other than he was staying at the hotel in the casino. See what you can find out. I want to know if he's still in town or if he's left, and if so, where he went."

"Will do," Mac said as he stood up and walked over to the door. "I assume you'd like this ASAP."

"Mac, have you ever known any information a cop wanted not to be ASAP?" Jeff responded.

"No, but thought I'd see if this was a first," he said with a grin as he walked out the door.

A moment later, the phone on Jeff's desk rang. "Detective Combs, this is Dr. Lindell, the coroner. I have the autopsy report on Lance Kendrick. I just finished it and knew it would be something you'd want immediately."

"Thank you, Doctor. Was his death caused by fentanyl, which you'd assumed based on what was found in his hand at the scene of his death?"

"Yes. It was exactly what I thought. It appears to me that the murderer jerry-rigged a fentanyl patch to make one that was so potent it caused Lance's death almost directly on contact. The fentanyl dosage in the patch on the decedent's hand was four times the amount that would be needed to kill a man his size. That, along with his asthma, and he never had a chance."

"I see. Did you find out anything else I should know?" Jeff asked.

"No. Except for his asthmatic condition, he was in good health and had no physical issues. It's pretty much a cut and dried case of being killed by an overdose of an opioid, in this case fentanyl."

"I appreciate the call, Dr. Lindell. It was what we expected, but obviously my job is to find out who put the patch in his hand and right now there aren't many suspects. But that's my problem, not yours. Again, thanks," Jeff said as he ended the call.

At 2:30 that afternoon there was a knock on his door and it was Mac.

"Good afternoon, Mac. Have any luck?"

"Yes, sir. It appears that Mr. Chen and his wife have returned to China."

"You're kidding. When I talked to the dealer and a couple of the other people who played poker on a somewhat regular basis in the high rollers room, they indicated he'd been playing there for the past several nights."

"That's true, but it seems his departure was sudden. I was able to find out that Lily Chen checked out of the hotel about 11:00 that night. Evidently she'd hired a town car, because after she checked out, she got in one that was waiting by the valet stand. The driver put quite a bit of luggage in the car."

"Okay, that takes care of her. What about John?"

"I had a long talk with the valet and he told me that at about 2:00 a.m. John Chen came running out of the casino and got into the same town car, only Lily wasn't in it. It left immediately."

"Got an idea where it went?"

"Yes. The valet said he'd talked to the driver several times while the driver was waiting for Mr. Chen. The driver told him that he had taken Mrs. Chen to the private airport just outside of town. She'd chartered a large jet and was planning to leave for China as soon as her husband got there."

"Sounds pretty sudden. Did the valet say anything else?"

"He said the driver told him that Mrs. Chen cried quietly all the way to the airport, but she never told him what it was about. He assumed that it was a family emergency. I also talked to the people at the airport and the jet that Mrs. Cheng chartered took off exactly at 2:27 a.m. The flight plan filed with the control tower was for China with a stopover in Hawaii to refuel. That's about it."

"Nice job. From what you found out, he was in the air when Lance was murdered, which means we can take him off the list of suspects, a list that was small to start with and is rapidly dwindling. No wonder the department pays me the big bucks," Jeff said sarcastically. "They expect me to pull a suspect out of thin air with a motive and a guarantee that they did it. Swell."

"Sorry, sir. If there's anything else you'd like me to do, let me know."

"I will, Mac, and thanks again."

CHAPTER FIFTEEN

Jeff was sitting at his desk contemplating his next move on the case when his secretary buzzed him. He pressed the intercom and said, "What can I do for you, Nina?"

"Sir, there's a woman on the phone who says it's very important that she talk to the lead detective about the gambler's murder. I know how busy you are, so I tried to pawn her off on one of the other detectives, but she wants to speak with you."

"No problem, Nina. I'll take the call. Thanks."

He picked up the phone and said, "This is Detective Jeff Combs. How may I help you?"

The voice on the other end hesitantly said, "Detective, I think I've found out something that might help you with the gambler's murder."

"I can use all the help I can get," Jeff said. "And you are?"

"My name is Becky Wilson. Before I tell you about it, I need to know something."

"All right. What is it?"

"If someone is an illegal immigrant and they tell law enforcement that they might be able to identify a murderer, would the fact that they're an illegal immigrant cause problems for them? And would anything happen to them if they had to go to court and testify against a defendant?"

"Becky, that's a very fair question and from it I'm assuming that the person you're calling on behalf of is an illegal immigrant. However, let me make something crystal clear. The fact that someone is an illegal immigrant has absolutely nothing to do with witnessing something and then reporting to law enforcement authorities what he or she saw."

"What if the case went to trial and the person was called to be a witness?"

"It would be like mixing apples and oranges. The fact that someone is illegally in the country has absolutely nothing to do with them witnessing something that was involved in a crime.

"As a matter of fact, if the defense attorney was stupid enough to even bring it up, the prosecuting attorney would object immediately and the judge would rule that it was irrelevant, which it is. I can absolutely assure you that the legal status of the person would not only not be an issue, it would not even be brought up."

"Thank you, Detective," Becky said. "Just a moment." She put her hand over the phone and Jeff could vaguely hear her talking to someone in Spanish. In a moment, she came back on the line.

"Now that we've gotten that out of the way," Jeff said, "why don't you tell me about what this person witnessed. Let's begin with a name."

"It's my cleaning lady. Her name is Juana Ortega. I'm her only private client. She works at the hotel at the casino, cleaning rooms. So many people gamble during the early morning hours that she works five days a week there from 11:00 p.m. to 7:00 a.m., when the hotel guests are generally out of their rooms and gambling in the casino."

"Those would be brutal hours for me, but I can see where a hotel that caters to gamblers would need people to work those hours. How does she fit you in?"

"She comes directly here from the hotel on Wednesdays. She's off Wednesday nights and Thursday nights, so this gives her extra income and then she can catch up on her sleep on the days that she's off work at the casino hotel."

"Again, I think that would be brutal, but I admire hard-working people, and she seems to be one."

"She is. I saw her briefly this morning when she came to my home and then I had to leave. I had several appointments as well as my monthly lunch with my mother and sister. I got back home about an hour ago, and I could tell something was wrong with Juana. I asked her what it was, and she said it was nothing.

"I knew that wasn't true, so I kept after her to tell me what it was. Finally, she broke down and started sobbing. She said if she told anyone, she would be deported. Her husband had told her that. I won't bore you with the details, but I was able to get her to tell me what it was that was bothering her."

"That must have been stressful for you," Jeff said.

"Yes, it was. Anyway, she was at the hotel working Monday night. She was getting some supplies out of the cleaning closet when she noticed a man walk down the hall, stop in front of a door, and knock on it. She said he had a bottle of champagne in one hand.

"Juana tells me stories from time to time about some of the more colorful people that are guests at the hotel, and originally she thought this might be one of them."

"That doesn't surprise me at all."

"A man opened the door and this is where it gets interesting. She had a very good look at the man who opened the door and it was the man who was murdered, the gambler. She saw a photo of the man on TV last night when she was watching the news before she went on her shift."

"Can you tell me more about the man who knocked on his door? What time was it?"

"Yes. I asked Juana the same thing and she told she'd looked at her watch just before she saw the man coming down the hall, because she wanted to make sure she was keeping to her schedule. She said it was 4:20 a.m.

"Anyway, she watched as the gambler opened the door. He smiled and the other man stuck his hand out to shake the gambler's hand. The gambler took a step back into the room and fell down. The other man closed the door and hurried towards the stairway exit steps, not the elevator. She thought that was strange. She also thought it was odd that he hadn't given the gambler the champagne he had with him."

Jeff could feel his adrenalin start to flow. "Becky, if I showed Juana several photographs, could she identify the man she saw knock on the gambler's door? Would you ask her?"

From the muted voices he could hear, he assumed that Becky had put her hand over the phone receiver and was talking to Juana. She came back on in a moment and said, "Yes, she thinks she could."

"I'd like to talk to her right now. Would it be alright if I come to your house?"

"Certainly. She'll be here for two more hours. Here's my address," she said.

Jeff wrote it down and said, "You're close by. I'll be there in ten minutes. One more thing, Becky, does Juana speak good English?"

"No, hardly any at all."

"Do you speak Spanish?" Jeff asked.

"Fluently, and you?"

"Let's put it this way. I took one semester in high school and my teacher passed me so she wouldn't have to teach me again, so no. Nothing other than I can order a beer and that probably won't help here."

"Not to worry. I'll be your interpreter. See you in a few minutes."

CHAPTER SIXTEEN

Jeff drove into the driveway of the rambling red-tiled Southwest style home and figured that neither Becky Wilson nor her husband had any worries about where their next paycheck was coming from.

The gate had been opened for Jeff to drive in, and he couldn't help but be impressed by the home's desert landscaping of multiple rare water-resistant plants. The house was in perfect condition, as was the putting green off to the side of the home, the grass in stark contrast to the hills behind the home and the desert style front yard.

He walked through the immaculate courtyard with hanging succulent plants and thought that Becky or whoever was responsible for them would love the courtyard at the commune. He rang the doorbell and heard soft Tibetan chimes inside, announcing that there was a visitor at the front door.

A moment later the door was opened by an attractive woman in her forties, her tanned fit body speaking to many hours devoted to golf or tennis each week. She wore a short-sleeved apricot-colored silk blouse with matching slacks and gold sandals, accentuating her earrings, rings, and bracelets.

Definitely not a shortage of money in this house, Jeff thought.

She smiled at Jeff and said, "You must be Detective Combs,

please come in. I'm Becky Wilson. Thanks for coming on such short notice. Juana has been a wonderful employee, and I want to help her in whatever way I can."

"No problem, I just appreciate your call. But before we get started with that, I have to tell you that your landscaping is not only beautiful, it's some of the best I've ever seen in the Palm Springs area. I love it that you kept to drought resistant plants."

"Thank you, Detective," Becky said. "When people come to Palm Springs and see that we have over one hundred golf courses here, they forget that this is a desert with over 300 sunny days a year. In other words, it doesn't rain here very much, so the amount of water used for keeping the golf courses manicured is horrific. A complete waste of a precious resource, in my opinion. Really, it's one of my pet peeves."

"And yet you have a putting green on your property," Jeff said with a grin.

"Detective, I've been married a long time, and I've learned there has to be a lot of give and take in a successful marriage. My husband gave on the landscaping, and I gave on the putting green. It was a lot cheaper than a divorce, plus I've kind of gotten used to him," she said with a laugh.

"Let's go into the solarium," Becky continued. "Since it's winter, the sky begins to change about this time of day, and it's a perfect place to watch the colors on the hills. Juana is waiting in there."

Jeff followed her down the hall and into the room she called the "solarium." He had to agree with her. It was a perfect time of day to be in the three-sided glass-walled room as they looked out at the colors of the late afternoon sky playing against the nearby hills. Upholstered furniture in muted earth shades acted as a backdrop. The effect was absolutely beautiful.

At the far end of the room, seated in a cream-colored armchair, a thin Hispanic woman of about fifty was nervously twisting her hands as she watched them approach. She was wearing a white t-shirt, grey leggings, and tennis shoes. Her thick black hair laced with grey was pulled into a topknot.

Jeff walked over to her and said, "Juana, I'm Detective Combs, but please call me Jeff. Thank you for allowing me to come this afternoon. I know you've been concerned about your status here in the United States, but I promise you, it is not a problem."

He looked over at Becky and nodded. She then translated his words, listened to Juana's reply and said, "Juana thanks you and says she trusts you."

"Good, would you ask her if she's comfortable with me recording our conversation? And just so I'm perfectly clear on this, from now on, you'll translate what each of us says, right?"

"Yes, and be gentle with her. You can see how scared she is."

"I promise I will."

Becky smiled at him and after Jeff took out his recording device and activated it, he said, "Juana, would you tell me what you saw at the hotel where you work the night before last?"

She told him exactly what had happened which was essentially what Becky had told Jeff over the phone. When she was finished, he said, "I have several photos here. I want you to look at them and let me know if you recognize anyone."

He'd brought photos of John Chen, Mark Cohen, and three deputies in plainclothes whose photos he'd taken before he left the police station. Juana carefully looked at each of them and then, several minutes later, she pointed to the one of Mark Cohen.

"That is the man I saw knock on the door and later close it."

"Juana, this is very, very important. Are you absolutely sure?"

"I swear on my mother's grave that is the man."

Becky translated and then said, "That is the most sacred thing she could swear on. You can take it to the bank that picture is of the man she saw."

"Juana, why didn't you go into the man's room? You saw him fall down and the other man leave. Weren't you curious what had happened to him?"

"Detective, it was not my room to clean. If I'd gone into a room that was not mine, I would get into very big trouble. Maybe even lose my job. My family needs me to have this job. I could not lose it."

"Didn't you want to know why he fell down?"

"Yes, but not enough to lose my job."

"Why did you tell Mrs. Wilson what you saw?"

She picked at her pants and looked out the window. Finally, after a long pause, she answered. "I saw something on the Spanish language television station I like to watch about a man being murdered at the hotel at the casino. The man's picture was on the television and the man who was talking about him asked if anyone knew anything about the murder, would they please contact the police department. I was torn, but I could not do that."

"You were afraid of what might happen to you, is that it?"

"Yes, very. Like I said, my family depends on me, but I am very sad about what happened to that man."

"I can see that."

"Yes. Every time I close my eyes, I see that man who murdered him. I had to tell someone. It was eating me up inside."

"Juana, is there anything else you can tell me about what you saw?

You may not think something is important, but it may turn out to be critical to the case."

She was quiet for a long time and then she said, "No, nothing. I have told you everything I know. Detective, will that man go to jail?"

"I certainly hope so, but I still need more evidence. What you have told me has been a huge help. I absolutely know that the man you saw is the murderer. Now I have to find more proof, and trust me, Juana, I will. Thank you so much for having the courage to talk to me.

"When I find more evidence, and the man is charged with murder, he may go to trial. If that happens, I will need your testimony. But Juana, I promise you that your status here in the United States, or the status of any member of your family, will never be mentioned."

He turned to Becky and said, "Thank you so much for calling and allowing me to come over here on such short notice. It's people like you and Juana who help keep the words law and order from being just words. Again, thanks."

"Happy to do it, Detective. My father was a lawyer, so I know how important evidence can be. What will you do now?"

"Quite honestly, I'm not sure. I know you've heard the term 'smoking gun.' Well, I know we have the right man, but now I need to find the smoking gun."

Becky stood up and Jeff said, "You stay and enjoy the play of sunset colors on the hills. Please reassure Juana that nothing will happen to her or her family. I'll let myself out, and again, thanks."

CHAPTER SEVENTEEN

Jeff got into his car and began the drive home to High Desert and whatever John's guinea pig experiment would be for dinner that evening. He was halfway home when the Bluetooth in his car rang, indicating he had a telephone call.

"This is Detective Combs," he said.

"Detective, this is Jack Michaels, over at the crime lab. Sorry to be so late getting back to you. Unfortunately, we were really short-staffed, and I just got around to it. Again, sorry."

"I understand. Those things happen. Did you find out anything from the fingerprints I sent you?"

"Yes. I understand the fingerprints came from the door as well as the fentanyl patch that was found in the victim's hand. We do have a positive match. His name is Mark Cohen."

"Is it a solid match?" Jeff asked.

"Couldn't get much more solid, Detective. You can take it to the bank with this one."

"Thanks for calling me. I know it's late, and I'm sure you're ready to leave your office. I really appreciate it. When you get a little time in the next day or so, would you please send me the formal results of the fingerprint analysis?"

"Not a problem. Hope the information helps. Go get the bad guy, Detective. Talk to you later."

Jeff pulled his car into a turnout and called the police station. When the phone was answered he said, "This is Detective Combs. Is Detective Stewart still there?"

"Let me check, sir. Just one moment," the young male voice said. He came back on the line a moment later and said, "Yes, sir, he's here. Would you like to speak with him?"

"Please."

A moment later he heard, "This is Mac, Detective, how can I help you?"

"Mac, I just got a call from the crime lab. Prints were taken from the hotel room door and the fentanyl patch found in the victim's hand. They came up with a solid match. The guy's name is Mark Cohen. I know it's late and if you have plans, I'll push this on to someone else, but I'd like everything you can get on this guy. If you can't do it, pawn it off on one of the other detectives and tell them I said it's high priority. I'd like the findings sent to my email. I'll pick up the results on my laptop. Any questions?"

"No, and I'm happy to do it. Matter-of-fact, I really didn't want to go home. Won't bore you with the details, but my girlfriend moved out and it's a little lonely there. Said she couldn't live with me any longer not knowing whether I'd be coming home on my own or in a body bag."

"Nice graphics," Jeff said.

"Yeah, I know. Kind of says it all about our relationship. Bottom line is she couldn't live with my line of work. She gave me an ultimatum. It was either her or my job. One guess which one I took. Enough of my drama. I'll get right on this, and I should have something for you in an hour or so."

"Sorry about your girlfriend. Our dangerous way of life isn't for everyone, and it may sound trite, but probably better to know that now than down the road when you have a couple of kids."

"Yeah, sounds good on paper, but doesn't feel real good right now."

"No, I'm sure it doesn't. But speaking as a man who has gone through a divorce, that doesn't feel real good either. Again, Mac, I'm sorry and thanks for doing this. I'll look forward to seeing what you come up with."

*****

When Jeff got to the compound, he called one of his deputies at the police station and asked who the on-call judge was for tonight. He was hoping it was one of the judges he had a good relationship with, and he'd approve Jeff's application for a search warrant for Mark's hotel room. He knew he still didn't have the smoking gun, but he hoped the results of the fingerprint analysis and Juana's statement would be enough for the judge to grant a search warrant.

When he got the name and number, he placed a call to Judge Kemptor's cell phone, glad he was on call, because since his son was with the police department, he was known to grant its members a little leniency when it came to issuing search warrants.

"Judge Kemptor speaking," the voice on the other end of the telephone line said.

"Judge, this is Detective Jeff Combs with the Palm Police Department. I would like to request that a search warrant be issued for the hotel room of a male individual by the name of Mark Cohen."

"Why are you requesting the search warrant, Detective?"

Jeff briefly described the facts of the case to the judge and then said, "The crime lab came back with results that showed Mark Cohen's fingerprints were found on the hotel door where the deceased victim was staying, as well as on the fentanyl patch in the victim's hand. The coroner declared the cause of death to be an overdose of fentanyl.

"I have recorded testimony from a witness who saw Mark Cohen at the victim's door at the time of the murder. Additionally, that witness saw the victim open the door and Mark Cohen reach out to shake the man's hand. The victim, Lance Kendrick, fell backwards to the floor immediately after they shook hands. the witness saw Mark Cohen close the door to the room and leave by way of the emergency stairs."

"That's pretty circumstantial, Detective. What are you hoping to find?"

"Ideally, I'd like to find some fentanyl in his room."

"And if you did, would you arrest him?"

"Yes, I would."

"You've not made mention of a motive, Detective. Are you hoping to find one?"

"Of course. I have one of my men pulling up everything he can find out about Mark Cohen. All I have right now is that he's a very wealthy gambler who plays high stakes poker games in casinos for a few days and then moves on. I'll know more later."

"When were you planning on executing the search warrant, if I grant it?"

"I would hope tonight."

"Do you think he'll be gambling tonight?"

"I don't know, but I think I can find out."

"All right. I'll grant the warrant as soon as you submit a signed affidavit to me by fax or email. You already have my contact information. I'll fax the search warrant to you. Where do you want it sent?"

"I just got home, so if you'd fax it to my machine in my home office here, that would be great. And thanks Judge Kemptor, I really appreciate this. Here's the number."

"Happy to help and hope the bench warrant produces the evidence you need. I've been watching this one because my wife and I like to go to the casino from time to time. I've always been curious about that high rollers room, but I knew I wasn't a good enough player to step into that arena. Plus, those stakes are a little rich for my blood, me being a state employee."

"Me, too," Jeff said.

CHAPTER EIGHTEEN

Laura was laying in her bed late at night. She'd been sleeping but now she was wide awake. She'd never had an out-of-body experience quite like this, and although she was very aware of her psychic abilities, this was new territory for her. She felt like she was actually in a dream, but she knew she wasn't.

It was as if Laura were a ghost or an invisible being that had no substance. She was in a guest suite at the casino hotel and she watched as a well-dressed handsome man walked into the room. He walked over to the kitchen counter in the suite and pulled a bottle of Veuve Clicquot champagne that was sitting on the counter towards him.

Then he went into the bedroom and over to his suitcase. He opened a manila envelope and pulled out what looked like a patch, a plastic glove, and a small brown medicine bottle.

Laura drifted closer to him and saw that the patch had a red side and a purple side. He put on the glove and pulled off the purple side, using his gloved hand, thus exposing an inner yellow side. He sprinkled something from the medicine bottle on the yellow side of the patch. Then he carefully reapplied the purple side of the patch over the yellow side. He walked out of his bedroom and put the patch next to the champagne bottle.

The man pulled the glove off, stuffed it in his pocket, and opened the door of his suite which had the number 246 on it. He looked both ways down the hall, but since it was 4:20 in the morning, no one was there. He walked down the hall to the supply closet, opened it, and threw the glove in a trash bin. He came back to his room and Laura heard him say to himself, "It's show time."

He picked up the bottle of champagne and the patch and walked over to the door leading to the hallway. "Just a guy carrying a bottle of champagne. Anyone sees me, I'm getting ready to celebrate the night's winnings," he said as he walked down the hall to the elevator. Laura was an invisible spirit moving next to him. They entered the elevator and rode up to the 4th floor.

As they left the elevator, the man deftly removed the purple liner of the patch he was holding and attached the red side of the patch to the piece of tape he'd applied to his hand before he left his hotel suite. Then he and Laura walked down the hall to room 475.

Laura noticed a cleaning lady at the far end of the hall peering out at them from a supply closet, but the man was so intent on what he was doing, Laura was sure he didn't see her.

The man knocked on the door of room 475 and a few moments later it was opened by the occupant, who seemed surprised to see the man who was standing in his doorway. Then he smiled, noticing the bottle of champagne the man had in his hand.

"Congratulations, Lance. Nice job tonight," he said as he stuck his hand out to shake hands. Seconds later Lance fell back on the floor, the patch adhering to his hand. The man quickly closed the door, walked to the emergency stairs and went down them to the second floor. He was back in his room in less than two minutes, Laura tagging along with him the whole time.

When the door was closed behind him, he pumped his fist in the air and said, "I rule. I'm king of the gamblers." He poured himself a stiff drink, downed it, and went into the bathroom.

Laura came out of the daze she was in and looked around, realizing she was back in her bedroom in the compound in High Desert. What she'd just experienced was a paranormal happening like none she'd ever had.

She knew the man in room 246 was the person who had killed Lance Kendrick, but what good would it do to tell people? There was no way her account of the murder would be believed by anyone, and yet, she was certain that what she'd just witnessed was true.

The only thing she could do was tell Jeff about it, and he'd have to find the evidence to support her vision or whatever it was. Maybe he'd be able to find the manila envelope with the medicine bottle and patches in it. She'd read a little about the opioid crisis and knew that a very strong opioid, fentanyl, had been responsible for a number of accidental overdose deaths in the last couple of years.

She had a feeling from what she'd seen that's what was in the envelope. Certainly, the way Lance had fallen to the floor, almost instantly, would fit in with what she'd read about the rapid onset of death from an overdose of fentanyl.

Laura tossed and turned, finally falling into a fitful sleep near dawn. She never set an alarm because she always woke up promptly at 6:00 a.m., but not this morning. When she woke up, she saw sunlight streaming through her window, and she immediately knew it was much later than 6:00 a.m.

She looked over at the clock on her nightstand and saw that it was 8:00. Laura threw off her covers, decided to forego a shower and rushed out of her house minutes later, planning to call Dick when the office opened and tell him she was running late. Her conversation with Jeff would have to wait until that evening.

CHAPTER NINETEEN

"Diego, please come join me," Lupe called into their bedroom where Diego was getting ready to go to the casino for the start of his shift as a dealer in the high rollers private card room.

"It's so beautiful out here by the pool tonight, it's almost magical. I've lit candles, and I'm having some champagne to celebrate how lucky I am to be with you. I know you never drink before you go to the casino to work, but one glass won't hurt you."

Diego walked out of the bedroom dressed for work in a starched white shirt, black pants, and a black cumberbund. The high rollers room was the only one in the casino where the dealers had to wear cumberbunds. Management felt that not only did the cumberbunds set the high roller dealers apart from the other dealers at the casino, it also fit in with many of the players in that room who often wore tuxedos.

"Ah, Lupe. You know there's nothing more I'd like to do than stay here with you and drink champagne, but the pit boss has a nose like a hound dog. He'd be able to smell it on me from six feet away, then he'd fire me, and we'd be broke," he said as he sat down in a lounge chair next to her.

"Diego, I've been thinking. I've never been happier than I have been with you these last few months. I know we said we'd never talk about anything long-term, just living together in this beautiful house was enough, but I've grown to love you. I never thought I'd say that I want to get married, but now I do. Diego, I want to have your baby. I want us to be a family."

He looked over at her in complete disbelief. She was the woman his family and his friends had told him he was crazy, loco, for even thinking a beauty like her would be interested in him.

When he met her, Lupe was working as a hostess at the steakhouse restaurant in the casino. She had the biggest, brownest eyes he'd ever seen. She was a beauty, but it was her eyes. When you looked at those eyes, it was like falling into an endless deep pool.

Once he'd looked in them, he'd never recovered, and several months later she'd quit work and now she was living with him. He knew his friends talked about her beautiful body and her long black hair, but for Diego, those were secondary. It had always been her eyes.

He looked in them now and all he wanted to do was stay with her tonight, hold her, and show her that she had just made him the happiest man in the world.

She swung her legs around so she could sit on the edge of her chaise and said, "Diego, did you hear what I just said? I want to marry you and be your wife."

"Lupe, are you sure? I never dared hope for such a thing. You know how much I love you. Yes, yes, yes. You have just made me the happiest man in the world."

He quickly stood up from his lounge chair and knelt down in front of her. "I want to do this right, Lupe. Lupe Escobar, will you marry me?"

"Yes, Deigo, yes." She kissed him deeply and then said, "When shall we get married?"

"As soon as we can. It will have to be a big wedding, because our families are so big. How long will it take to plan a big wedding?"

"I will start making lists tonight of things we have to do. When you come back from the casino, you can look at the lists with me, and then we can decide. Oh, Diego, this is the happiest day of my life. I'm going to call my parents and some of my friends and tell them."

"Don't you think it's a little late, Lupe? It's already 11:30."

"It's never too late for good news, and this is the best news ever. When will you be home? We can celebrate with champagne, and I'll even make some goodies to go with it."

He knew John Chen expected him to get rid of Lance tonight, but that would have to wait until tomorrow night. Nothing was going to spoil tonight for Lupe and him. And having murder on his hands would definitely do that.

CHAPTER TWENTY

It was dark and the courtyard in the compound was truly magical with little flickering lights on every tree and bush. John had put three large pillared candles on the table. As if by some silent invitation, the residents of the compound gathered around the table, looking forward to sharing the events of the day and whatever John would be serving.

"Here you be," John said as he handed glasses of wine to everyone but Marty. "Tonight, we're having steak with anchovy garlic butter, Brussel sprouts wrapped in bacon with a balsamic honey glaze, a salad, and garlic bread. And before anyone says they don't eat anchovies, I want you to just try a little dab of the special anchovy butter to see if you like it.

"In the last few years a new taste has become popular. We've only known the four basic tastes, namely sweet, sour, salty, and bitter. Anyway, it's sweeping the nation and it's called umami. It's kind of a savory taste and has pretty much been officially adopted by chefs around the country as the fifth taste. It's great."

"Seriously, John, anchovies? I dunno. I'm not sure I can handle that. Could you put mine on the side?" Les asked.

"I can, but trust me. Once you taste it, you'll be piling it up on your steak," John said.

Everyone added their two bits on anchovy experiences and they were pretty divided as to who liked them and who didn't. Jeff noticed that Laura hadn't said a word during the interchange and wondered why she was being so uncommonly quiet.

"Laura, you haven't said a word since you sat down. I know we've all had interesting days, and I want to hear about everyone's, but why are you being so quiet?" Jeff asked politely.

Laura took a sip of her wine and then said, "Jeff, I had an out-of-body experience early this morning, and it's pretty relevant to your murder case."

"Uh-oh, I've been down this road before," Marty said, rolling her eyes.

"Actually, you haven't, Marty," Laura said. "This was a completely new experience, even for me."

"Well, since I can use about all the help I can get on this case, and I'll tell you where I'm at with it in a little while, I'd like to hear about your experience," Jeff said

"Jeff, if I told you while I was having this out-of-body experience, or whatever you want to call it, that I was with a man when he murdered Lance Kendrick, what would you say?"

Jeff was in the middle of taking a sip of wine which immediately sputtered out of his mouth. "Let me see if I heard you right. You just said you were with a man when he murdered Lance Kendrick. How come you never mentioned it to me before now?" he asked a bit sarcastically.

"I just found out this morning and this is the first time I've seen you since then." She paused and looked around the table, then she said, "Guys, stay with me here. Like I said, I've never had an experience like this before and quite frankly, I'm not even sure what to call it. It was something psychic, but I don't know exactly what it was."

"Laura, for Pete's sake. None of us needs the experience to have the perfect description attached to it. Just tell us what in the heck happened," Les said.

"Okay, here goes. It was the early morning hours…" she began and then told them what had happened in great detail. When she was finished, she sat back, looking around the table. There was a stunned expression on everyone's face.

She reached down and petted Patron who had walked over to her when she'd begun to speak. His hackles were up and he stood next to her the entire time while she spoke. Laura put his head between her hands and spoke softly to him in what Marty always said was their "private mumbo-jumbo" talk. A moment later the big dog became calm and laid down at her feet.

Jeff was the first to speak. "I believe you, Laura. Like you, I have no idea what to call it, and as you know, that kind of testimony would never stand up in a court of law, but you've at least given me some tangibles on where this man in Room 246 at the hotel might have his fentanyl supply stashed. That fits in with what a witness told me."

John held up his hand and said, "Hold off until I get back. Max just indicated that dinner is ready. Give us a couple of minutes to get it on the table."

It was very quiet as everyone started eating. A few minutes into the dinner John couldn't resist and said, "So Les, I notice you've spooned the anchovy butter all over your steak. Guess that means you like it."

"In a gazillion years, I never thought I'd be eating anchovy butter and Brussel sprouts and wondering if I could have more. I don't know if I qualify, but I'm beginning to think I've become a gourmand," Les said.

"Then I take it the two dishes are a hit?" John asked, looking around the table for confirmation. Seeing the satisfied expressions on everyone's face he smiled and nodded at Max. "Guys, you just have to trust me when I bring something new and unusual to the table. Have I ever let you down?"

There was a chorus of noes and it became quiet again as they continued to eat. Marty was the first to break the silence.

"Jeff, I went to Carl's this afternoon and talked to him. But before I tell you what he had to say, I have to tell you what his little Maltipoo, Miss Simone, was wearing today. Picture a little fluffball dog in a pink silk body suit with white mink cuffs on her legs."

"No, my mind refuses to even entertain that thought," Jeff said. "Are you sure it was mink? No one wears mink in Palm Springs. Not with the temperatures we have here."

"Miss S. does because according to Carl, he keeps his office, where she sleeps on a pink satin pillow, at 60 degrees when she wears her furs. From that I gathered she has similar fur-lined outfits."

There was a stunned silence at the table and then Max said, "Marty, are ya' jes' playin' with us? Guys I know would laugh 'til they was layin' on the ground if'n they ever saw some dog in pink silk and mink. Ain't normal if ya' ask me."

"Max, I'm sure there are a lot of people who would absolutely agree with you, but trust me, I'm telling you the truth and it was quite a sight."

"Yeah, a sight fer bustin' a gut," Max said.

With that, all of them continued to quietly eat their meal, knowing that Jeff would say something when he was ready about the results of his investigation.

CHAPTER TWENTY-ONE

"Well, I guess it's my turn," Jeff said as he finished the last bite on his plate and laid his fork across it. "It's been beyond an interesting day. First of all, I found out what happened to John Chen, and Marty, you were absolutely right about him not being in the high rollers room last night. He had to leave suddenly for China."

"For China? Really?" Laura asked. "Why?"

"Yes, one of my men was able to find out his wife chartered a plane to fly them to China. He left the casino about 2:00 a.m., was driven to a private airport, and as soon as he got there, the plane left for China. That means he was well on his way out of the country when Lance was murdered that night, which makes the suspect list smaller and smaller."

"What was the reason for the sudden trip?" Les asked.

"That we don't know. My man found out that the driver who took Mrs. Chen to the airport told the valet at the casino that Mrs. Chen cried the whole time he drove her to the airport. Whether it was a family emergency or something else, we don't know."

"When a man is accustomed to winning big most the time and then leaves suddenly, it must have been something very serious," Laura said. "I'm getting vibes that it had to do with his wife's health."

"If it was her health, it must have been pretty serious for her to charter a jet. The officer who was doing the work for me was curious what the cost of something like that would be. He said the best he could come up with was an estimate of chartering a jet from Los Angeles to Shanghai, and that was around $155,000."

"Wow, sure would put a dent in his previous winnings," Marty said.

"Agreed, which makes me think it was something very, very serious, but we'll probably never know. The crime lab called and confirmed that Mark Cohen's fingerprints match the ones on Lance's hotel room door and on the fentanyl patch."

"Can you arrest him for the murder because of the fingerprints?" Les asked.

"Unfortunately, no. Any defense attorney worth his salt would get that case thrown out of court. I was able to get a statement from an eyewitness who saw Mark knock on the victim's door and can place Mark at the scene of the murder when it happened."

"How did you find the eyewitness?" John asked.

"I wish I could say it was because of incredible sleuthing on my part, but I can't," Jeff said.

He started to tell them how Becky had called him and then said, "Sorry guys, I'm going to have to leave you hanging. I have a bell attached to my fax machine, and I just heard it ring. I'm expecting an in-depth report on Mark Cohen. I'll be back shortly."

He quickly walked over to his house and went into his office where he pulled the report out of the machine, sat down at his desk, and spent the next several minutes examining it. The report was thorough, going back to Mark's early schooling.

Mac had attached a note stating that a lot of the information contained in the report had come from a report that had been prepared by a pit boss at a casino in New Jersey. Evidently Mark had won big four nights in a row and there was some concern by the pit boss that he was cheating in some way.

The report had been written by the pit boss who was also a psychologist. He had left his practice after one of his patients had committed suicide, and he'd gone to work at the New Jersey casino as a pit boss, so the report contained psychological conclusions as to Mark's personality and gambling.

The conclusion of the report by the pit boss was that Mark did not cheat, but he was simply very, very good at gambling. He did give a personal opinion that Mark could not tolerate losing. He referred to Mark as having a "hypercompetitive complex," meaning he was over-the-top competitive. Winning was simply an extension of his ego. He could not allow himself to lose when he was gambling, because it negated his sense of who he was.

The psychologist-pit boss had gone on to write that people like Mark were latently dangerous, meaning that if his need for winning was not met, he could become violent. The pit boss cited several instances in psychology journals where this need for winning or being the best was so strong that when one of these people lost, it had resulted in them murdering the person who had caused them to lose.

The report went on to list Mark's assets, which were huge, and painted a picture of a very wealthy man. He generally played in casinos five nights a week, changing his location every few days. He wasn't married, and from the report, had no significant other.

Mac had done an incredibly good job in a short time, even interviewing several people Mark had gambled with over the years. Each of them had said Mark defined himself by his gambling ability and on the rare instances he lost, became obsessed with beating whoever had won.

One of the people interviewed said he'd witnessed Mark berate a man who had won and then walked away from the table with his winnings. Mark had followed him outside the casino and demanded that he return to the card table to play so Mark could win. He called the man a wuss and a few other uncharitable names.

The man who had been interviewed said he was a professional gambler and had run across Mark in several different casinos throughout the United States. He said Mark rarely lost, but when he did, he became consumed with playing against the person again and winning. He told Mac he was sure shrinks had a word for someone who had to be the best at everything, because that's what it looked like to this man.

The report on his family background indicated Mark was the black sheep of the family, a family who lived in a large gated estate in upstate New York. His father was the founding partner of one of the largest law firms on the East Coast. His brother had followed in his father's footsteps, and his sister was a doctor and the Chief of Staff at a prestigious hospital in Connecticut. His mother was on the board of several well-known charitable organizations and often referred to in the newspapers as a "socialite."

The report indicated Mark had little to do with his family and vice-versa. It went on to say that there had been no known visits from Mark to his family since he'd left home when he turned eighteen. The report indicated that he had no known circle of friends and referred to him as a classic loner.

The report concluded by saying he had no police record other than a few parking violations and speeding tickets which had been paid.

Jeff reread the report in its entirety and then sat back in his chair digesting what he had read. He was most interested in the psychologist-pit boss' portion of the report.

From what the man had written, and it seemed he really had been a psychologist from the degrees he listed, it was his opinion, documented, that men who possessed the "hyperachievement complex" were capable of murder. The very fact he'd included information about that complex in his report indicated to Jeff that he felt Mark was capable of murder.

This was one more notch in the circumstantial belt of evidence that was accruing against Mark Cohen, but Jeff still needed something more. He had enough to arrest him, but he knew the District Attorney would say there was not enough evidence to get a conviction. That was Jeff's job. He knew it was up to him to find the "smoking gun."

CHAPTER TWENTY-TWO

After reviewing the fax from Mac, Jeff walked out into the courtyard and back to his friends. They were all quietly waiting for him, entranced by what he'd been telling them.

"Was your fax information helpful?" Marty asked.

"Yes, it certainly confirms everything I've been thinking about Mark Cohen, but I still don't have enough for a conviction.

"Jeff, when you left a little while ago, you'd just started telling us about a phone call you'd received. Was that relevant to the case you're building?" Les asked.

"Extremely. I met with a woman who can place Mark at Lance's door at the time of his murder."

"How did you ever find her?" Marty asked.

"Actually, she came to me. Here's how that happened." Jeff told them about Becky's phone call to him and the subsequent meeting he had with Juana Ortega at Becky's home.

"Jeff, was she a small Hispanic woman who wore her hair in a bun?" Laura asked.

"Yes, why?"

"She was in my dream or whatever you want to call it. She was the woman at the far end of the hall peering out of the supply closet."

"Laura, I'll never doubt you again. That's exactly where she told me she was when she saw Mark knock on Lance's door. I wish I could use your account, but not only would the District Attorney think I'm crazy, he'd probably tell my chief about it, and I'd be out of a job."

"Yes, sometimes having this gift is really frustrating, like now. I know what I saw really happened, but who would believe it?"

A chorus of "We would," rang out through the courtyard.

"Thanks, guys. I really appreciate it. Since you're so supportive, I'll keep telling you what the whatevers are giving me. Jeff, the one thing I am getting is that you need to get into Mark's room and search it, particularly to look for that manila envelope.

"You said something about a 'smoking gun' and it would sure seem to me if you could find the fentanyl in Mark's luggage, that would be it. Seems pretty hard to refute," Laura said.

"I agree, but I would have to search his room when he's not in it and that could be a problem. I don't want to get into his room and find he's asleep or whatever. I haven't quite figured out how to do it."

"Jeff, I just got an idea, and I think it will work. It would involve the woman I told you about, Marie, and her dog. I know you don't like anyone to know about projected searches, but I'm sure this woman could be trusted. Laura, any thoughts on this?"

Laura was quiet for several long moments, and then she said, "I'm getting a feeling that the woman is extremely honorable and can be trusted implicitly. I don't know exactly what your idea is Marty, but I hope it involves her dog. The dog can confirm that Mark's aura is such that he's capable of murder."

"Laura, what's an aura?" Max asked. "Ain't never heard of one of them before."

"It's a quality people have that surrounds them. It can only be seen by someone who has extra sensory perception. What makes it important, and I have seen it many times, is that if someone has a very light or even a golden aura, that person is thought to have divine protection and is enlightened. The colors of the rainbow all indicate certain things."

"What would a red aura indicate?" John asked, clearly unfamiliar with auras.

"A red aura is one of the most powerful colors found in aura energy. It represents the life force, passion. To accurately assess someone's red color, you'd need to see where on the red spectrum it is."

"Laura, I hear ya', but I think this is way beyond me," Max said.

"No it's not, Max. Think about it. If you saw a dark, dark red, you'd feel quite differently than if you saw a light color of pink. The dark red would be at the far end of the spectrum, or passion misused. A light pink would be a joyous passion. It really does make sense."

"Okay, Laura, thanks for the aura lesson. Now where does this apply to me?" Jeff asked.

"If someone were to see a very dark red or even a black aura around Mark, that would indicate that he's definitely capable of murder or could have even murdered."

"That's all well and good in theory, Laura, but I still fail to see who's going to tell me the color of Mark's aura."

"From what Miss Olive's owner told Marty, her dog has an ability to sense when someone is, for lack of a better term, a bad person.

Carl also told Marty a story about her dog sensing that a customer in his store was going to steal something. The dog may not see auras, but apparently she has some extra sensory power that allows her to assess a person's character."

"Jeff, what I have in mind is exactly that and it will also help you find out where Mark is, so you can search his room. Let me go make a phone call and then I'll explain the whole plan to you. Trust me, this will work. I'll be back in a few minutes," Marty said as she stood up and walked towards their house.

"Laura, can ya' look at me and tell me what my aura is?" Max said a moment later, as he tried unsuccessfully to suppress a snicker.

"Max, I decided several years ago that reading people's auras was kind of like spying on them. In an emergency, yes, I could, but I don't like to use my gift, if you want to call it that, for fun. I hope you understand."

"Sure, mine would probably be so crystal white pure it would blind ya' anyway," Max said.

"Probably," Laura responded.

CHAPTER TWENTY-THREE

Marty went into her office and opened the center drawer of her desk, looking for the card Marie had given her the day before.

I swear, she thought as she shuffled through the cards in her desk, *one of these days I'm going to be so organized that I'll immediately put someone's name and contact information on the contacts list of my cell phone so I never have to resort to doing this again.*

When she found the card, she punched Marie's numbers into her phone and a moment later she heard Marie say, "Hello?"

"Hi, Marie. This is Marty Morgan. I met you and Miss Olive at the coffee shop in the casino yesterday."

"Yes, of course. How did your appraisal go last night?"

"It was fascinating. Beautiful things, but that's not the reason I'm calling. I need your help."

"Well, I have no idea what this is about, but if I can help you with something, of course. What is it?"

"I actually need your help and Miss Olive's help," Marty said.

"Now you've made me really curious, but before you take the time to tell me what you need, I must tell you that I know nothing about Native American things."

"Marie, it has nothing to do with my appraisal. I think I mentioned that my husband is a detective with the Palm Springs Police Department. He's the lead detective investigating the gambler's murder we briefly discussed."

"I've seen some things on television about it and wondered how that was coming along. I noticed that the police department has asked for help. Does he have any suspects?" Marie asked.

"Yes, and that's why I'm calling. He's almost certain he knows who the murderer is, but while all the evidence points to this person, the evidence Jeff has isn't strong enough to bring about a conviction. In other words, he has enough to arrest the person, but he's concerned the District Attorney will say it's not enough evidence to go to trial and get a conviction."

"All right, but I fail to see what any of that has to do with Miss Olive or me."

"Jeff was able to get a judge to issue a search warrant for the suspect's hotel room, but the problem is knowing when the suspect will be in his room. Here's where you come in.

"I was thinking that if you and Miss Olive were in line at the high rollers card room before it opened, obviously you'd be able to see who else is in line. If the suspect, and I'd email you a photo of him, was in the line, I'd like you to walk up to the guard and make some kind of small talk, like how many people he expected tonight or some such thing.

"That would mean you would be walking by the people waiting in line. If the suspect is in line, I'd like you to assess Miss Olive's reaction to him. You told me that she freezes up when she comes near someone evil or whatever you want to call it."

"I'm more than willing to help. I'm sure Miss Olive and I can do that," Marie said.

"There a second part to it," Marty said.

"Okay, what's that?"

"I would want you to stick around long enough to make sure the suspect goes into the high rollers room to gamble. I'd assume if he's in line that would mean he's going to gamble, but I need you to make sure. Then I'd like you to go back into the main casino and text my husband that the suspect is in the high rollers room. That would allow Jeff to search the room while the suspect is gambling. Do you think you could do that?" Marty asked.

"Are you kidding? To be part of a murder investigation with the police department? This may be the most exciting day of my life. I'll have to give Miss Olive a bath right now in case your husband wants to take our picture or something, so she'll look good."

"Marie, I don't think that's going to happen, but who knows? Probably better to be safe than sorry."

"Let's see. I'll need to wear something that looks good on camera or television in case someone wants to interview me. I understand a lot of politicians wear blue when they're going to be on TV."

"Think about it, Marie. I rather doubt that Jeff would admit that his wife contacted someone who had a dog with ESP and that's what enabled him to solve the murder."

"Yeah, you're probably right. Well, when it's all over can I tell people. My sister will just die when she hears about it."

"Marie, since we're dealing with a murder here, I'm going to take that last sentence figuratively, not literally."

"I see what you mean. Well, let's just say she'll be super-excited."

"Good. I know that the dealers and the pit boss go into the high roller's room at 11:50 so they can set up and the dealers can put their personal items in lockers. The players aren't allowed in until midnight. When do people start lining up at the door?"

"Marty, these are people who don't like to wait in line. Whenever I've been there, I've never gotten there before 11:45 and I've always been allowed in the room. There are some slot machines at the far end of the casino, almost in the hallway that leads to the high rollers room. We'll play there and as soon as we see people beginning to line up, we'll do the same."

"That sounds good. Let me go over it again with you. When you see Mark, he's the suspect, you walk up to the front of the line and say something to the guard, like 'How much longer?' If you could even pause in front of Mark for a moment, and maybe reach into your purse like you're getting your phone or something, you could get a very good sense of Miss Olive's reaction to him."

"I will."

"Marie, when we talked yesterday, you mentioned that Miss Olive stiffens up. What, specifically, does she do?"

"It's hard to explain, Marty. When she stiffens up, there's a strip of her coat that runs down her back that stands up like what I've seen on guard dogs, think they're called hackles. Secondly, her whole body becomes rigid. I mean if you touch her, she's like a marble statue."

"And that's what she did at the car wash."

"Exactly. If this Mark guy is the murderer, I'll bet she does it when she gets near him."

"I feel so certain that he's the murderer, I'm sure she'll have that reaction. Here's my husband's telephone number. When you text him about Mark being seated in the room, also text him that Miss Olive became stiff when she was next to him. I'll fill Jeff in on what that means. Any questions?"

"No."

"I have a guard who will escort me into the room at 11:50. I'll pass right by you and Miss Olive, but I won't acknowledge you. Mark has no idea that my husband is a police detective."

"Marty, when this is all over, would you let me know what happens?"

"Of course, particularly considering you and Miss Olive are playing such a big part in it."

"Well, I better go. I can't wait to tell my husband what's going on and Miss Olive and I need some time to get ready. What is it they say in show business to wish someone good luck? Think it's 'break a leg.' You can wish that for us."

"Marie, Miss Olive, break a leg," Marty said with a laugh. "See you in the line."

CHAPTER TWENTY-FOUR

When Marty returned to the courtyard she said, "Jeff, I solved your problem about knowing when Mark would be in his room."

"Great. How did you do that?"

She told him about her conversation with Marie and how she would be texting Jeff when Mark was sitting down at a table in the high rollers card room.

"Good thinking, Marty. That should work. I'm sure there's nothing about a woman carrying a dog in her purse that would alert him to anything. Women carrying dogs in their purses are pretty common in Palm Springs."

"That's what I thought. Now what?"

"I'm going to call one of my deputes who's been very helpful with this case. I'll pick him up and he can go to the casino with me. Back in a minute," he said as he stood up and headed towards their house.

*****

"Mac, this is Detective Combs. I'm sorry to bother you, but I was able to get a search warrant for Mark Cohen's room at the casino hotel, and I'd like you to go with me when I search his room."

"Not a problem, sir. Matter-of-fact I welcome anything that takes me out of my apartment and away from my thoughts about my ex-girlfriend. This is good timing. Why don't I meet you at the station and you won't have to spend time finding my apartment?"

"That would help, thanks. I'll meet you there at 11:30 tonight. I have someone who will be watching to make sure Mark is playing poker in the high rollers room."

"If we find something, are you planning on waiting for him in the room and arresting him when he come back?" Mac asked.

"I honestly don't know. I haven't gotten that far. What I'm hoping to find is the fentanyl. That should put the amount of evidence we have over the tipping point and convince the DA there's enough to go to trial. At least that's what I'm hoping."

"I'm ready. Let's do it. From that report I faxed you, this guy sounds like a real head case. Talk about controlling. And that shrink's report sure indicated the guy seemed to be capable of murder."

"My thoughts exactly. See you in a couple of hours."

*****

Something was bothering Jeff and he couldn't put his finger on it. He'd found in the past when that happened if he sat quietly and just let his mind do what it wanted, it would come to him. He knew Marty and the rest of the group was waiting for him, but he decided to take a moment and see if he could capture the thought that was eluding him.

He closed his eyes and took a couple of deep breaths. In a moment, he saw a clear glove. Jeff opened his eyes and tried to remember where he had recently heard something about a glove.

Then it came to him. Laura had told him that Mark had opened the supply closet door on the far end of the hallway next to the stairs, took his glove off, and then thrown it in a trash barrel in the closet.

He wondered how often the hotel dumped the trash cans in the supply closets. Juana would know.

He got Becky Johnson's card out of his pocket and called her. She answered on the first ring.

"Becky, this is Detective Jeff Combs. I'm sorry to bother you so late at night, but I've been able to get a lot more evidence against Mark Cohen. I'm hoping you can help me get one more piece of evidence. Would you call Juana for me and ask her how often the hotel dumps the trash barrels in the supply closets?"

"Sure, I'll do it right now. I know she has a problem sleeping on her days off because her inner time clock is geared to working nights. She told me recently that she stays up until about midnight and then tries to go to sleep. She said it's a real problem, because her husband is a gardener and has to be up at 5:30 in the morning. I'll call you right back."

Jeff sat at his desk looking through the report Mac had prepared to see if he'd missed anything. Within minutes, his phone rang.

"This is Detective Combs," he said.

"Detective, it's Becky. Juana said the trash in the supply rooms at the hotel are picked up every day, but in slow times it's every other day, or sometimes every three days. She said right now is a slow time and she knows that the trash was picked up early the night Lance was murdered and it won't be picked up again until tomorrow night."

"That's great news. I believe there's something that Mark put in one of the trash barrels and if I can find it, it sure would help me with this case. Thanks again for your help."

He immediately called Mac and said, "It's Detective Combs. Change of plans. Can you meet me at the police department in fifteen minutes?"

"Sure. On my way."

Jeff hurried back to where everyone was sitting at the table in the courtyard and said, "I've got to run. Marty, it's a go with Marie. Laura, I got to thinking about the glove you saw Mark put in the trash barrel in the supply closet. The trash hasn't been dumped, so Mac, one of my deputies, and I are going to check it out. I think the term for doing this is called 'dumpster diving.'

"I didn't have the heart to tell him that's why we're going to the casino early. I found out from Juana that in slow times they don't dump the trash in the supply closets every day, so I have a little window of opportunity. Wish me luck!"

He leaned down and kissed Marty and then looked over at Laura. "Oh, great seer, any words of wisdom for me?"

She was quiet for a moment and then said, "Neither you or your deputy will be in danger. I'm getting a picture of a trash can dumped upside down and a plastic glove at the very top. Since it's at the top I think Juana was right. It was dumped just before the glove was put into it."

"Thanks, Laura. Let's hope your words go from your lips to God's ears, and I get lucky with it. See you all tomorrow."

Words of "good luck" and "be careful" rang through the courtyard as Jeff walked over to the gate and out to his car.

CHAPTER TWENTY-FIVE

"Thanks for meeting me on such short notice, Mac. I really appreciate you being here. I didn't have the courage to tell you what the change of plans are. There's a trash barrel in a supply closet at the hotel casino that we need to search for a plastic glove that I believe was used by Mark when he was working on the fentanyl patch. It should have his prints on it as well as traces of fentanyl."

"Sir, would I be out of line to ask where you got that information?" Mac asked.

Uh-oh, Jeff thought. *How far do I go telling him that we're looking for trash and searching Mark's room for a manila folder because of a psychic who saw the glove and the fentanyl? After this, Mac just might put in for a transfer.*

"Mac, let me ask you something. Have you ever had any experience with psychics or paranormal things?"

He was quiet for several moments and then said, "Kind of. My sister has what my family has always called 'the gift.' She knows when things are going to happen. We all used to laugh at her, but so many things have happened that she foretold, that now we all listen to her.

"As a matter of fact, if she says to do it, we do. If she says don't, we don't. A couple of years ago a woman I was seeing and I decided to do one of those champagne sunset balloon rides. I thought it would be romantic, and I happened to mention it to my sister. She told me not to go. She said I'd be hurt."

"What happened?" Jeff asked, glancing over at Mac.

"I wish I'd listened to her. The balloon was tethered to a heavy cable. Somehow it got loose, swung around, and hit me in the head. I fell to the bottom of the gondola, unconscious, and the balloon took off.

"The guy who was in charge of our balloon was in contact with some guy on the ground and eventually he was able to make an emergency landing. I don't know what happened between when I was hit and when I woke up in a hospital room with a huge bump on my forehead the next morning. I was there for two days so the doctors could monitor me and make sure I didn't have any lasting injuries. Fortunately, I didn't."

"Sounds like you were lucky," Jeff said.

"I was, but you want to hear the topper?" Mac asked.

"Sure."

"The owner of the balloon company came to the hospital and gave me two gift certificates so my girlfriend and I could take another balloon ride whenever we wanted."

"You're kidding. What did you tell him?"

"I tore up the certificates and told him I was expecting all my medical bills to be paid in full and compensation for my pain and suffering, as well as my girlfriend's. He left. Guess he thought a free balloon ride would make up for everything."

"What did your sister say?" Jeff asked.

"What do you expect? 'I told you so' a number of times. But I will tell you that now everyone in the family pays attention to Cissy. So, I guess that was a long answer to your question. And why the question? Kind of out of the realm of police work, isn't it?"

"I know, so here's the deal. My sister-in-law is psychic, and she had a dream or something or other about Mark. She says it was like she was with him from before he killed Lance to afterwards. Here's what she told me," he said as he recounted Laura's experience to Mac.

"Well, based on my sister, could be," Mac said. "That gene skipped me. I take it we're going to look for the manila folder. What else?"

"Here's the part that might not thrill you. I told you about the plastic glove. Laura, my wife's sister, told me that it's at the bottom of the trash barrel. I checked with a maid and she told me that during slow times the trash is not dumped daily and that trash barrel will not be dumped until tomorrow."

"Oh, man. Are you going to tell me that we're going dumpster diving?"

"No. We're simply going to turn the trash barrel upside down and Laura said that the glove should be on top of the contents after we dump them."

"Okay, Detective, but I sure hope she's psychic about where the glove is. I have no idea why, but I have nightmares about getting stuck in some trash bin. Think it comes from all the times I've been involved in undercover drug busts and the perp has thrown his stash in some dumpster, and I've had to go in and find it. You wouldn't believe some of the disgusting things people throw in a dumpster. It's a real downer."

"Yeah, I remember those days, and not with fondness," Jeff said as he pulled into the hotel parking lot. "First stop is the manager to get permission to go through the trash."

"Great, just great," Mac said.

CHAPTER TWENTY-SIX

As Jeff walked up to the casino hotel reception desk, he noticed the hotel was quiet at this time of night, most of the guests having checked in earlier. "May I help you, sir?" a young woman asked.

"Yes, I'm Detective Jeff Combs with the Palm Springs Police Department. I'd like to speak with the manager." He showed her his badge.

"The only manager we have on premises at this time is the night manager. Would you like me to call him?"

"Yes, please."

A few minutes later a man in his 30's walked out of a door behind the reception desk and up to the desk where Jeff was standing. "My name is Rick Bellamy. May I help you?"

"Yes, Mr. Bellamy. I'm Detective Jeff Combs. This is in relation to the murder that occurred here in the hotel two nights ago. I have a tip that there is some evidence in a trash can in the supply room on the second floor. I'd like to see it."

"Not a problem, sir, but we have two supply rooms on each floor. The trash from the rooms is put into barrels in the special trash room. Those barrels are dumped daily. The ones in the supply closet are only dumped a couple of times a week. Would you happen to know which supply room on that floor it is?"

"Yes. The supply room that is closest to the exit stairs."

"Certainly, sir. I can escort you there."

"I appreciate your offer, but I think the fewer people the better. Is the door to that room unlocked?"

"Yes, sir. Take the elevator to the second floor. Turn right and it's the last door on the right. As you said, it's next to the stairs."

"Two more things, Mr. Bellamy. If I need to take something from the trash as evidence, do I need to clear it with you?"

"No, sir, that will be fine."

"Secondly, I have a search warrant to search the room of one of your guests, Mark Cohen, signed by Judge Kemptor. Here it is. It authorizes me to search room 246. I'll need a key card to access that room."

The manager turned to the young woman and told her to get a key card for that room. A few seconds later she gave it to him, which he, in turn, gave to Jeff.

"Sir, I do have one request," Mr. Bellamy said.

"Yes, what is it?"

"If you're going to make an arrest or there are any problems, would you please try to handle them quietly? We've had enough bad publicity, and I'd hate to add to it."

"I can't completely promise you that, Mr. Bellamy, but we'll certainly do the best we can. If we're dealing with a murderer, which I believe we are, outcomes can be a little unpredictable. I'll let you know when we've finished up and are ready to leave, arrest or not."

"Thanks, I'd appreciate that."

Mac and Jeff turned around and headed for the elevator. They rode it up to the second floor and easily found the supply room, grateful no one was in the hallway. They entered the room, closed the door, and turned on the light.

"That must be it, sir. Looks like it's the only one in here. There are handles on the sides. I think if we each take one, we should be able to turn it over easily, but I'm wondering if we should put a sheet on the floor, so we don't make a mess."

"Good idea, Mac," Jeff said as he reached up and pulled the top sheet off a nearby stack. He spread it on the floor. "Okay, on three. One, two, three," he said as they tipped over the can.

"Looks like your sister-in-law was right," Mac said. "Here's the glove, just like she said, right on top."

Jeff put a glove on his hand, took the glove that was presumably Mark's, and put it in an evidence bag.

"Now what, sir?"

"Mac, I've got 10:30 on my watch. My contact is going to text me about midnight and let me know if Mark's in the high rollers room. It doesn't open until midnight. You've got a couple of choices. We can go out to the car and wait until I hear from her or we can go down to the casino, play the slots, and watch the action."

"I'm a lousy gambler, but I love the mind-numbingness of the slots. Let's go to the casino."

"That's fine. One caveat. We need to pick a couple of slots that are next to where you think Mark would walk on his way to the poker room."

"Not a prob. Follow me."

Jeff carefully opened the supply closet door, looked from side to side, and seeing nothing, gestured for Mac to follow him. They walked down the hall to the elevators, and no one who saw them would suspect that the bearded man with the earring and the large man wearing a golf shirt, shorts, and a knee brace were anything other than a couple of men on their way to the casino.

CHAPTER TWENTY-SEVEN

Jeff and Mac were standing side by side playing the nickel slot machines at the far end of the casino when Jeff quietly said, "There's Mark. Looks like he's on his way to the high rollers room." He glanced at his watch which read 11:45. "Look down the hall and tell me what you see, Mac."

"He got in line in front of a room that has glass walls. It looks like he's about third back from the front of the line," Mac said.

"Look down there from time to time and let me know what's happening," Jeff said. He knew Marty would be arriving any minute and he didn't want her to acknowledge him. He looked the opposite way from where Mac was looking, hoping to silently convey to her with a nod indicating "no," that she was not to acknowledge him.

Two minutes later he saw her with an armed guard escorting her into the casino. He kept looking at her and when she saw him, he nodded. She understood and walked by him and went down the hall. A moment later a woman with a dog in a large purse walked down the hall. He assumed that was Marie, the woman who would be texting him in a few minutes.

He kept playing the slot machine and quietly said to Mac, "Start to slow down. We should be getting a text in a about ten minutes. If we're a go, I want to head up to his room immediately. I understand that he usually gambles in the high rollers private card room until it closes at 4:00 a.m."

"Not a problem. As you heard when my slot machine went ding-ding-ding, I won a $100 jackpot a little while ago, so I think I've used up my luck for the night."

Jeff felt his phone vibrate in his pocket and he pulled it out. Marie had texted *He's sitting at the table. Miss Olive went stiff.*

He texted back, *Thanks.*

"It's time, Mac. Let's go."

They quickly walked through the casino to the tower where the hotel rooms were, rode the elevator up to the second floor, and walked down the hall to room 246. Jeff inserted the key card the manager had given him in the lock.

When they were in the room, Jeff closed the door and locked it. "I brought gloves for you, Mac. Put these on. I'm going to search his bedroom. I want you to see if you can come up with anything on his laptop or his iPad."

"Will do," Mac said, taking the gloves from Jeff.

Jeff walked into the bedroom and stood there for a moment, looking around as he pulled on a pair of latex gloves. He spotted Mark's suitcase on the luggage rack at the end of the bed and walked over to it. He opened it and looked in the pouch on the raised side of the suitcase, hoping to see a manila envelope.

He spotted a file folder inside the pouch which he quickly removed. When he opened it, he saw that a manila envelope had been inserted inside it. "Please be here, please be here," he said out loud as he opened the metal clasp on the envelope.

He looked inside the envelope and saw several what appeared to be medical patches. He also found a brown medicine bottle with white powder in it. He assumed the patches and the white powder in the bottle were fentanyl, but he'd need the police crime lab to confirm it.

"I found what I think is the fentanyl, Mac. I've bagged it. That's the main thing I was looking for. You find anything?"

"I can't even get into his email. His whole computer is password protected and I've had no luck with the run of the mill passwords. Be nice if I knew his wife, girlfriend, and dog's names."

"Why?"

"Because those are the usual passwords people use, or some combination of them. Guess I'm just out of luck. You got any ideas?"

"None. That's why I usually bring someone from our cyber-crime division if something's going to involve a computer."

"Okay. What now?"

Just then Jeff felt his phone vibrate, indicating he had a new text. One part of him thought it was a really odd time for someone to be texting him, but the other part of him wondered if it had something to do with Mark.

He took his phone out of his pocket and looked at the text. It simply said *Mark sick. Hide. M*

"Mac, Mark's on his way. Get behind the drapes in the room where you are, and I'll hide behind the bedroom drapes."

CHAPTER TWENTY-EIGHT

Mark had been waiting in line for the doors to the high rollers room to open for several minutes. His stomach felt queasy and he wondered if he'd eaten something at the expensive dinner he'd had at the hotel's specialty steak house that didn't agree with him. He didn't think that was it, given that the restaurant was the only one in Palm Springs to be given a Michelin star, but he knew anything was possible.

At precisely 11:50, three guards, three dealers, a pit boss, and a woman walked up to the doors of the private card room and the guard unlocked the doors, admitting them. He saw the woman and one of the guards walk over to a table in the back of the room. The woman put her camera and a briefcase on the table, and then took a number of items out of the briefcase.

The dealers went to their lockers and then to their tables, got the decks of cards and the shoes from beneath the tables, and set them up for play. The pit boss circulated among the tables, watching to see that the dealers weren't doing anything unusual.

While he was waiting to be let into the room, Mark noticed a woman with a dog in her purse walking towards the guard at the door. She paused, standing next to him for a moment, while she petted the dog, and then she continued on towards the guard. They talked for several moments and then she walked back to the end of line.

I can't stand dogs, Mark thought. *The last thing I need when I don't feel good is to have one anywhere near me. As allergic as I am to them, that's not going to make me feel any better. Maybe I should just pass on playing tonight.*

As he stood there deliberating what he should do, the guard opened the doors and the two people in front of him went into the card room. He decided to ignore his stomach and sat down at one of the tables. Within minutes, the tables had filled, and the door guard told the people in line that they'd be admitted when there was a vacancy at one of the tables.

Mark played for forty-five minutes and then said, "I'm out." He pulled the sizable pile of chips towards him and put them into a casino bag the dealer handed him. He gave a $100 chip to the dealer as a tip and said, "Thanks. I don't feel so good. See you tomorrow night."

He stood up and walked out of the room. The guard let an attractive woman into the room who walked over to the table Mark had left and sat in his chair. "Hope this chair still has his luck in it," she said with a laugh as she put her chips on the table.

Marty was examining a piece of pottery that Carl had attributed to the San Ildefonso Pueblo and dated back to the 19th century. She knew it would be difficult to find anything comparable to get a sense of its value.

Although the card Carl had written said the piece was in excellent condition, she automatically ran her own finger test, a test she'd been taught by her mentor many years ago. She fondly remembered the curmudgeonly old man, and she could hear the words he always told her as clearly as if he were standing next to her.

"Marty, you have to pick up the piece, close your eyes, and run your fingers all over it, because your eyes will lie every time when you want a piece to be in perfect condition." His sage advice had been responsible for her finding flaws in ceramic pieces many, many times.

She closed her eyes and began the finger inspection.

She was concentrating so hard she didn't realize for a moment or so that Jerome was talking to her. "I'm sorry, Jerome. I was in another world here, a pretty old one. What was it you said?"

"Just said the way that guy won last night, I'm surprised he quit playing so early."

"Who?" Marty asked as she looked around.

"That guy we were talking about last night. You know, the one who had all the chips. Heard him say he wasn't feeling well."

Marty whirled around and saw that Mark was gone. All she could think of was that Jeff and his deputy were in his room and Mark was headed there. She reached into her pocket where she kept her phone and quickly sent a text to Jeff that read *Mark sick. Hide. M*

She turned to Jerome who was looking at her oddly and said, "I just thought of something I needed to tell my husband. Okay, back to work."

"You texted your husband at 12:50 at night? I didn't know detectives stayed up that late. I thought they had to get a good night's sleep so they could catch the bad guys," Jerome said with a laugh.

He's trying to catch the bad guy, Marty thought, *and I just hope I was in time.*

CHAPTER TWENTY-NINE

I don't know when I've felt this bad, Mark thought, as he rushed to his room. *I just hope I can make it there before I toss my cookies.*

A moment later he slipped his key card into the lock on his door and dashed into the bathroom. Jeff could hear him from where he was standing behind the drapes and realized the reason he'd left the game was that he was sick.

Even though the bathroom door was open, Mark's back was to him, so Jeff was able to hurry into the living room and pull the drapes back from where Mac was hiding. Mac had his gun drawn, ready to shoot if it had been anyone other than Jeff. "Mark's sick," Jeff whispered. "You take the right side of the bathroom door, and I'll take the left. I'll do the talking."

With his gun in his hand, Jeff walked back into the bedroom, Mac next to him. They flanked the bathroom door. There was no reason to hurry because Mark was violently throwing up.

When Mark became quiet, Jeff said in a loud voice, "Police, Mark. You're under arrest for the murder of Lance Kendrick."

Mark turned around to acknowledge them, but then turned back towards the toilet, throwing up again. Mac and Jeff both kept their guns on him. Jeff said, "Mac, read him his Miranda rights while I call the station. As sick as this guy looks, I'm going to have the paramedics come along with our guys. I'm also going to open the door for them, so they don't break it down."

Within minutes there were several policemen and two EMT's in Mark's hotel room. Mark was handcuffed and strapped down on a gurney. "Guys, I want this done quietly," Jeff said. "Anyone asks you what's going on, just say the man was very sick and had a large amount of cash in his possession. The police are with him for protection. I promised the manager I'd keep things as quiet as possible. Take him to the hospital. I'll meet you there."

"Sure thing, Detective. See you in a few minutes."

As Mac and Jeff approached Jeff's car, Jeff asked Mac to drive. He said he had a couple of calls he had to make. First, he called the hospital. He told the emergency room doctor that a man who was under arrest was being transported there and was quite sick.

Jeff told the doctor there was a chance the man had been exposed to fentanyl and might be ill from it. He told him he had the substance the man had been exposed to and would have the police crime lab run a test on it first thing in the morning. He said he'd be at the hospital momentarily.

Next, he called the hotel and asked to speak with Mr. Bellamy. "I really appreciate your help tonight. I left the key card in the room. My deputies have impounded all of Mr. Cohen's belongings and will take them with them when they leave his room.

"Although the room is vacant, I think there's a very good chance that an opioid called fentanyl was in the room and Mr. Cohen became very ill from possible exposure to it. I would suggest you tell your cleaning crew to be sure and wear gloves when they're cleaning his room. I also think it might be a good idea to destroy the bedding, towels, and anything else, like glasses he might have drunk from. I'm sure this isn't the first time something like this has happened."

"Thanks, Detective. I saw the ambulance and the police presence.

I overheard one of them telling a bystander they were just there because he'd won a lot of money. Thanks for your discretion. I'm taking it there's a lot more to the story than what you've told me."

"Yes, there is. But that will do for now. Again, thanks for your help," Jeff said as he ended the call.

Jeff sat back, clearly tired, as Mac drove them to the hospital. "Detective, I'll bet your wife worries when you're on a job like tonight," Mac said.

"Oh, no!" Jeff said. He hurriedly got his telephone out of his pocket and texted Marty. *Everything's ok. Mark's on his way to the hospital. Mac and I are fine. Thanks for the heads up. See you in a couple of hours.*

He turned to Mac and said, "I am so glad you said something about Marty. She's the one who texted me that Mark was on his way to his room."

"How would she know anything about that?" Mac asked, clearly perplexed.

"She's an antique and art appraiser and has been in the high rollers room the last two nights appraising their collection. She must have noticed that Mark was gone and that's why she texted me."

"She's the one who sent the text that Mark was in the card room at the beginning of the game?"

"No, it's a bit more complicated than that. I'd tell you, but you've probably had enough psychic stuff for tonight. Anyway, don't think it will help us fill out the paperwork we have ahead of us."

"You're the boss. One good thing came out of all this. Didn't think about my ex-girlfriend once," Mac said.

"Well, saving your own life has a way of keeping your priorities where they should be," Jeff said with a grin.

EPILOGUE

Several nights later the compound residents were assembled at the table in the courtyard, ready to discuss the day's happenings and catch up with each other. John and Max had been on catering events the last two nights and everyone had done their own thing for dinner, mainly some rendition of fast food. They were eagerly awaiting a good meal, as they were tired of fast food fare.

"I feel like I've been completely out of touch," John said. "I saw something on the news where your murderer had been captured and then died, but just then my oven timer went off and by the time I was able to watch television again, the news guy was on to something else. I'd like to hear the real story."

"He died?" Max asked.

"Yes," Jeff said. "Here's what happened," and he told them about the events that led to Mark's capture. "Obviously, what I found in the manila envelope was fentanyl and Mark died after too much exposure to it."

"Kind of fitting, if you ask me," Laura said. "And it sounds like my dream or whatever you want to call it, helped you, not only with the envelope, but also with the glove."

"Trust me, Laura," Jeff said. "I will be forever beholden to you and I want you to know that I've been a believer for a long time, but this one was way over the top. I honestly don't think a case against Mark would have made it to trial without you."

"Kind of interesting how things work out. If I hadn't been appraising in that high rollers room, Mark would have gotten to his room and found you and your deputy. Who knows what would have happened then?" Marty said.

"True, but from what I saw of Mark Cohen that night, he was lucky he made it back to his room."

"And what if I hadn't met Marie Wilson and Miss Olive in the coffee shop? They certainly helped. Everything was kind of serendipitous."

"Seren… what?" Max asked. "That's a purty big word. What does it mean?

"It means that what seem to be random things happening for no apparent reason are really just psychic phenomena that we all need to be aware of," Laura said.

"Laura, we all know you have the eye or gift or whatever you want to call it," Les said. "We love you, but don't push it."

"And on that note, Max and I will begin to serve you more kinds of finger foods than you could ever imagine, compliments of our catering clients, who were both going out of town and insisted that we take the leftovers. And knowing our beloved compound residents and their appetites, we said sure and thank you!"

RECIPES

AMAZINGLY MOIST SALMON

Ingredients:
4 salmon filets, 6 oz. ea.
3 tbsp. mayonnaise
2 tbsp. Dijon mustard
1 tsp. lemon zest
Nonstick cooking spray

Directions:
Preheat oven to 500 degrees. Combine mayonnaise, mustard, and lemon zest in a small bowl and spread mixture on salmon filets. Apply cooking spray to baking sheet, place salmon on sheet, skin side down and bake 10-12 minutes until filets flake easily and have an internal temp of 120 degrees. Remove and serve. Enjoy!

BACON AND CHEESE JALAPENO POPPERS

Ingredients:
8 jalapeno peppers, approx. 3-4" long
1 8 oz. block cream cheese, room temperature
1 cup grated sharp cheddar cheese
¼ tsp. garlic powder

¼ tsp. onion powder
¼ tsp. salt
¼ tsp, pepper
¼ cup finely chopped cilantro, plus 1 tbsp. for garnish
¼ cup green onions, finely sliced, plus 1 tbsp. for garnish
4 slices bacon, fried crisp and crumbled
2 tbsp, feta cheese, crumbled
1 handful Kettle Brand Country Style Barbecue potato chips

Directions:

Preheat oven to 425 degrees. Line a large cookie sheet with parchment paper for easy clean-up. Cut each pepper in half lengthwise. Use a small spoon (a serrated grapefruit spoon works great) to scoop out the seeds and membranes from each pepper and discard. Cut off and discard the thick top part of the pepper (about ¼ of an inch) and the stem. The half pepper will be open at the top part and taper to a point at the bottom of the pepper.

In a bowl, combine the cream cheese, cheddar cheese, chopped cilantro, green onion, garlic powder, onion powder, salt, and pepper. Stir to combine. Stuff the peppers with the cheese mixture (you might have a small amount left over), then gently press equal amounts of the crumbled bacon onto the top of the cheese mixture in each pepper. Bake for 10 – 13 minutes until the cheese is bubbling and starting to turn golden.

Meanwhile, place a big handful of barbecue chips on a dry cutting board and crush them into tiny pieces using a rolling pin. Place crushed chips in a small bowl. Add feta cheese, 1 tbsp. chopped cilantro, and green onion. Stir and combine.

Garnish the top of each pepper with the crushed chip mixture and transfer to a large flat serving dish/tray. Serve & enjoy!

Caution: The seeds inside jalapeno peppers are fiery hot and should not be touched with your bare hands or fingers. Avoid touching your hands or fingers to your face or eyes while cleaning the peppers. To be safe, I wear disposable latex kitchen gloves while cleaning the peppers. Wash your hands thoroughly with hot soapy water after you clean the peppers.

STEAK WITH ANCHOVY BUTTER

Ingredients:

1 steak, about 1 lb. (flank, hanger, strip or rib eye)
¼ cup oil-packed salted anchovies, drained
¼ cup red wine vinegar
2 small shallots, finely minced
1 cup unsalted butter, soft
Salt & pepper to taste

Directions:

Anchovy Butter:

Drain the oil off the anchovies and place them in small sauce pan with the vinegar and shallots. Cook over medium heat for about 5 minutes, until vinegar has completely reduced and shallots are very soft and translucent.

In a medium bowl combine the shallot mixture with 1 cup of softened butter. Using the back of a wooden spoon, crush the butter and anchovies into a soft mixture until it is fully combined and soft.

Set aside and apply half the mixture to the steak once it is almost finished on the BBQ or frying pan. Spoon the remaining half into a small ramekin and serve on the side.

Steak:

Season steak on both sides with salt & pepper and let sit 1 hour at room temperature. Cook the steak on the BBQ or else on the stove top in a heavy cast iron skillet in the usual manner. Enjoy!

NOTE: The recipe above makes a generous amount of anchovy butter, easily enough for 2 steaks.

BACON WRAPPED BRUSSEL SPROUTS W/HONEY GLAZE

Ingredients:

12 small Brussel sprouts (or 6 large, cut in half after microwaved)
6 strips of bacon, each strip cut in half
½ cup balsamic vinegar
1 garlic clove, minced
2 tbsp. honey
1 pinch dry rosemary
1 pinch garlic salt

Directions:

Honey Glaze:

Whisk balsamic vinegar and honey together in a saucepan over medium heat. Cook, stirring occasionally, until mixture begins to bubble, 3-5 minutes. Stir garlic, rosemary, and garlic salt into vinegar mixture.

Cook and stir until mixture starts to foam. Reduce heat to low and simmer, stirring occasionally, until glaze coats the back of a wooden spoon, about 30 minutes. Keep warm until ready to apply glaze to Brussels.

Brussels:

Preheat oven to 400 degrees. Rinse the Brussels, peel off the outer thick leaf, and discard. Place Brussels in microwave dish. Add ¼ inch of water. Cover dish with plastic wrap & seal tightly. Punch 4-6 holes in plastic wrap with a sharp knife point and microwave on high for 5 minutes.

Remove Brussels from microwave and let cool, then cut top off each Brussel. Place a wire cooling rack inside a rimmed baking sheet. Wrap ½ slice of bacon around each Brussel and place wrapped Brussels on wire rack with seam side of bacon on the bottom. Bake in oven for 20 minutes. Remove from oven and brush with honey glaze sauce and serve. Enjoy!

NOTE: I like to serve these Brussels as a side dish with steak, but they can also be served as an hors d'oeuvres. Either way, I stick a fancy cocktail toothpick in each Brussel so they can be eaten as finger food. That's why I prefer to use small Brussels.

HEATH BAR SHEET CAKE

Ingredients:
Cake:
2 cups all-purpose flour
3 tbsp. corn starch
1 tbsp. baking powder
1 tsp. salt
2 cups sugar
1 cup milk
½ cup vegetable oil
1 tbsp. vanilla extract
5 large egg whites
Nonstick cooking spray

Sauce & Frosting:
1 cup light brown sugar
½ cup milk
4 tbsp. unsalted butter
¼ tsp. salt
2/3 cup sweetened condensed milk
1 tbsp. vanilla extract
1 cup chilled heavy cream
2 Heath candy bars (2.1 oz. ea.) roughly chopped

Directions:
Preheat oven to 325 degrees & spray a 9" x 13" ovenproof baking pan with cooking spray. In a large bowl whisk together the flour, corn starch, baking powder, & salt.

In a medium bowl whisk together the sugar, milk, oil, vanilla, and egg whites until smooth. Pour the liquid ingredients over the dry ingredients and whisk until just combined.

Pour the batter into the prepared pan and smooth the top. Bake until pale golden brown, about 40 minutes.

While the cake is in the oven, make the sauce: combine the brown sugar, milk, butter, and salt in a small saucepan and melt over low heat. Increase heat to medium and cook, stirring often until the sauce thickens, about 8 minutes. Remove the pan from the heat and stir in the condensed milk and vanilla. Pour the sauce into a bowl and let it cool to room temperature or refrigerate until no longer warm.

Remove the cake from the oven and transfer to a wire cooling rack. Cool for 20 minutes, then using a ½" wide wooden dowel or the round end of a wooden spoon, gently poke holes in the cake so they go about ¾'s of the way deep into the cake. Space the holes about 1" apart from each other. Pour the sauce over the cake, and try to get most of it to soak into the holes in the cake.

In a large bowl, whisk the cream with an electric mixer until stiff peaks form. Scrape the whipped cream onto the cake and level it with a frosting spatula. Sprinkle the chopped candy bars over the cake and chill in refrigerator for a minimum of 1 hour before serving from the pan. Enjoy!

LEAVE A REVIEW

I'd really appreciate it you could take a few seconds and leave a review of Murder & High Rollers.

Just go to the link below. Thank you so much, it means a lot to me ~ Dianne

https://www.amazon.com/gp/product/B081LLZCLW

Paperbacks & Ebooks for FREE

Go to www.dianneharman.com/freepaperback.html and get your FREE copies of Dianne's books and favorite recipes immediately by signing up for her newsletter.

Once you've signed up for her newsletter you're eligible to win three paperbacks. One lucky winner is picked every week. Hurry before the offer ends!

ABOUT THE AUTHOR

Dianne lives in Huntington Beach, California, with her husband, Tom, a former California State Senator, and her boxer dog, Kelly. Her passions are cooking, reading, and dogs, so whenever she has a little free time, you can either find her in the kitchen, playing with Kelly in the back yard, or curled up with the latest book she's reading. Her award-winning books include:

Cedar Bay Cozy Mystery Series

Cedar Bay Cozy Mystery Series - Boxed Set

Liz Lucas Cozy Mystery Series

Liz Lucas Cozy Mystery Series - Boxed Set

High Desert Cozy Mystery Series

High Desert Cozy Mystery Series - Boxed Set

Northwest Cozy Mystery Series

Northwest Cozy Mystery Series - Boxed Set

Midwest Cozy Mystery Series

Midwest Cozy Mystery Series - Boxed Set

Jack Trout Cozy Mystery Series

Cottonwood Springs Cozy Mystery Series

Cottonwood Springs Mystery Series – Boxed Set

Midlife Journey Series

Midlife Journey Series – Boxed Set

The Holly Lewis Mystery Series

Holly Lewis Mystery Series – Boxed Set

Coyote Series

Red Zero Series

Black Dot Series

Newsletter

If you would like to be notified of her latest releases please go to www.dianneharman.com and sign up for her newsletter.

Website: www.dianneharman.com,
Blog: www.dianneharman.com/blog
Email: dianne@dianneharman.com

PUBLISHING 12/30/19

MURDER AT THE NEW DAWN B & B

BOOK NINE OF

THE COTTONWOOD SPRINGS COZY MYSTERY SERIES

http://getbook.at/MND

An unlikable guest
Who was abusive to his wife
A marriage in trouble
Someone thought he should be murdered
And he was.

Brett reminds Linc of a time when he could have prevented an abusive spouse from hurting his wife, a close friend of Linc's, and he's always regretted it. Did he regret it enough to do something about it years later?

Could it have been the B & B guest who found Amanda irresistible and her husband's treatment of her frightening? Or even her loving father, worried about his only daughter?

It's up to Brigid and Sheriff Davis to find out just how abusive Brett was and who murdered him. Plenty of dogs, recipes, and page-turning suspense in this, the 9th book in the Cottonwood Springs Cozy Mystery Series by a two-time USA Today Bestselling Author.

Open your smartphone, point and shoot at the QR code below. You will be taken to Amazon where you can pre-order 'Murder at the New Dawn B & B'.

(Download the QR code app onto your smartphone from the iTunes or Google Play store in order to read the QR code below.)

Made in the USA
Columbia, SC
21 December 2019

85524728R00090